CAUGHT

an Elite PR novel

CLARE JAMES

Entangled Publishing, LLC
2614 South Timberline Road
Suite 109
Fort Collins, CO 80525
Visit our website at www.entangledpublishing.com.

Brazen is an imprint of Entangled Publishing, LLC. For more information on our titles, visit www.brazenbooks.com.

Edited by Vanessa Mitchell
Cover design by Heather Howland
Cover art by Shutterstock

Manufactured in the United States of America

First Edition June 2015

To LJ,

For everything—it's been an amazing ride.

Chapter One

Holy shit, does this guy know what he's doing in the sack! Or in the bathroom stall, rather.

That was Vivian Blake's first thought as she watched the video. Watched as he slammed the voluptuous blonde against the wall and drove into her with so much force, it took Viv's breath away. Though she was watching the X-rated bathroom romp from her iPad—in the privacy of her own home—it didn't stop the heat from spreading over her chest, up her neck and face, to the tips of her ears. She felt downright pervy watching the footage. The surprisingly clear footage. Yeah, she could see everything. This was no shady production. The picture was clear and sharp, damn near HD. She sank a little deeper under her covers, the cool, crisp sheets brushing against her sensitive skin.

Viv couldn't help but wonder how she would feel up against that wall. *Ah*—she squirmed as another wave of warmth rolled in, blanketing her from head to toe, reaching places she hadn't felt in a long time. It was too much to even think about.

Get your mind out of your pants and focus, Viv.

The tendons in the man's arms bulged as he held Blondie up, cradling her thighs. It was one of the hottest things she had ever seen. And we were talking *arms* for fuck's sake. Once she locked in on his face? Forget about it. The camera was placed overhead so the angle provided Viv with an excellent view of that rugged mug. Piercing blue eyes, strong jaw with the perfect amount of stubble, and plump kissable lips that he used to his full advantage as he brought this unnamed woman to the brink of ecstasy in a bar bathroom.

The *guy*, however, had a name. A name worth millions. Mr. Bathroom Stall Sex Guy was better known as racing sensation Jarod Cage. And he was a foolish, foolish man.

The recording went viral almost immediately after he'd done the deed. What followed was a steady, and often vicious, stream of media coverage all over Racing Land. *Cage Caught Again. More Trouble for Racing Bad Boy. Could This Be the Beginning of the End?*

Now, twenty hours later, most of the photos and video clips had been taken down from the scummy websites. The attorneys made sure of it. But as a lucky insider, Viv had one of the few copies left for her viewing pleasure.

And what a pleasure it was.

As she assessed the evidence in question, it was easy to make out the delicious piece of mancake in the stall. Almost too easy. Viv wasn't even remotely into racing, yet she recognized the man on the screen as Jarod Cage. There'd be no way to deny it was him. She made a note to look into the logistics as soon as she could—the equipment used to get the footage, as well as the methods of distribution—to find out who was responsible for the leak.

PR Rule Number 1: Know your audience. That included your enemies.

Amazed that the guy could hold up this mystery woman for so long, Viv checked the running time on the video. Five minutes. She stroked her own flabby arms and grimaced. Then she typed "go to the gym" on her work calendar.

Jarod shifted his angle a bit, and the woman's blond locks fell over her full breasts. It reminded Viv that an appointment with her stylist was also in order. She could use some highlights in her hair for summer. She'd already been feeling frumpy lately, and this bombshell wasn't helping matters. Not that she wanted to ooze sex like Video Girl here—that would not go over well at the office—but she could stand to pump it up a notch. Maybe even start breaking into her collection of shoes, take them out for a spin every now and again. Viv was no Carrie Bradshaw, but she did have a few pairs of Manolos and Jimmy Choos from an off-season sale. She considered them an investment and cared for them like a comic book nerd cares for a first-edition *Batman* or his G.I. Joe action figure. It was true. In fact, her burgundy slingbacks had never even left the box. What a shame, when they could be digging into a fine ass like the one currently gracing her screen.

Another minute ticked by. Viv's brain finally, reluctantly, pulled away from Mr. Sex on Wheels and shifted to work mode. It was time for some serious damage control, and they would need to come up with the mother of all excuses for this one. Drinking problem? A bad reaction from prescription drugs? A doppelgänger? She'd have to cook up something good to get him out of this predicament.

How he didn't realize he was being recorded in this compromising position, she had no idea. Actually, that wasn't true. She did understand. After dealing with so many athletes, musicians, and actors—and their very delicate dirty laundry—she'd come to realize that incredible talent came with a price...intellect, in most cases. Thus, leaving the *other head* in charge of the important decisions.

No difference here. It was an open-and-shut case. Thankfully for the manwhore, it was Viv's job to clean up indiscretions like these and make him nice and shiny again.

And she wasn't above spinning the story, either. Whatever it took. She never would've made it as a lawyer, bound by all the rules and ethics. She was more of a rule *bender* than follower, an imperative strategy if they wanted to win in the court of public opinion.

The only court that mattered.

Viv paused the tape and zoomed in.

Was that a tattoo on his hip?

Jarod's jeans hung around his ankles, but she could only get a view of the black spot on his right side when he pulled away from Video Girl. And it was never long enough for a decent look. *Damn.* Though her skin was unmarked, Viv had an unhealthy obsession with ink. Particularly on hot, strapping men.

She pulled up her laptop and opened Jarod's file. It was going to take more than this sex show to see exactly what she was dealing with. Not that she really had a choice in the matter. Her boss simply emailed the file on the way out of the office and said, "Read up. Your new client will be here in the morning."

That was Miranda Wells—president of Elite Public Relations' Atlanta Group and world-class spin doctor. With one of the most impressive track records in the industry, Elite PR managed clients in major business, sports, and entertainment hubs around the world. The majority of the Atlanta Group's roster came from the Nashville music scene, Southern athletes, and actors. Miranda knew them all, and she was one woman you never wanted to piss off.

Viv knew that firsthand, which is why she'd hit this case hard to ensure she was more than prepared for her new assignment. Even if tomorrow was the day before the Fourth of July and technically a company holiday.

Who needed picnics and fireworks, anyway?

Viv didn't work sixty hours a week and move every eight to twelve months for the fun of it. She was there to learn. Recruited right out of college for Elite's executive track, she had worked stints in the Chicago, Philly, and DC offices before Atlanta. Her goal was to make it to the New York office by the time she was twenty-five, and then start planting some roots. That was the dream. Until then, everything else was just temporary.

But thanks to Miranda, she was already a year off schedule. Viv celebrated her twenty-sixth birthday last week… and it wasn't anywhere near the Big Apple. The timing of her next move was at her boss's discretion, and so far Miranda had rejected three of her transfer requests. "You're not ready," she'd said each time.

So Viv would do her job and repair the reputation of this latest exhibitionist. What was it with celebrities anyway? If she had a dollar for every sex scandal that came through Elite's doors…

Viv clicked through the notes and files of this latest PR nightmare, which included some very serious threats from Jarod's sponsor—the squeaky clean Saturn Corp. It was apparent that the leading American manufacturer of confectionery was not at all impressed by these recent events. As it turned out, chocolate and T-and-A didn't mix.

Thing was, if Jarod lost his sponsor, he would also lose his place on the NASCAR circuit and millions of dollars in endorsements. This was a career-defining moment for the driver. And if Viv played it right, she could restore Mr. Cage's image, protect his livelihood, and watch him win whatever it is that you win in racing.

Then she'd be a shoo-in for the New York transfer.

She made a quick detour to search for more information about Jarod's profession. What was it called anyway? A club? Pastime? Activity?

According to Wiki, NASCAR is a *sport*. Second only to the NFL in TV ratings, it held some major world attendance titles in sporting events. No wonder the sponsors were worried. The public had serious power in the racing world.

This wasn't going to be easy. Music, business, even baseball or football, were all in Viv's wheelhouse. But NASCAR? Let's be serious. She simply couldn't comprehend why anyone would think it was a challenge to drive around in circles all day. Or why people would pay to watch.

Didn't matter. This assignment was a chance to get *back on track*—see, she was already acclimating—but only if she did everything perfectly.

Eye on the prize.

She organized her paperwork and electronics, creating a makeshift office on her plush king-size bed. Viv loved working in her bedroom—a space that took up the entire top floor in her swanky loft. Soft blue tones covered the walls and seemed to soothe her after the long and grueling hours she spent in the downtown office. It was a cozy nest: a four-poster bed, floral prints, and an oversize puffy chaise. A stark contrast to the main floor, which looked more like a model home with the sleek furniture and modern art. There wasn't a hint of anything personal to be found. Viv rented the place fully furnished—except for the bedroom—and hadn't made one change to the place. She never did.

That was Viv, a walking contradiction. She recognized it, but it suited her. She could entertain and look the part of a successful businesswoman if she wished. And then, at the end of the day, she could curl up in her cozy bedroom with her cooking magazines, watch a romcom, or read one of her steamy romance novels.

Speaking of steamy, Viv turned her attention back to the video and hit play. Geez, the sounds that came from that little bathroom stall were enough to make a grown woman blush. Jarod was still going strong. My God, how long could he last?

A loud groan or growl—was it a growl?—echoed in her bedroom. She wasn't quite sure what that was, but Video Girl sure seemed to like it. And that only reminded Viv how long it'd been since she'd been manhandled.

Not that her experiences were anything close to this, and not that she'd wanted it like *that* anyway. Still…

Ever since she started at Elite, she'd had no time for a relationship. Men, even those with the stamina of an Olympic athlete and ass of a Greek god, were not part of her plan just yet. Why put down roots and get attached when she'd be leaving soon? And honestly, relationship and commitment or not, Viv wasn't a hook-up-in-a-bar-bathroom kind of gal. Though she had to admit, she was seriously considering changing her position on that hard-and-fast rule. Thanks in part to this showing of *Legally Boned* with Jarod Cage.

Thing was, even Viv's most determined suitors, like Jake at the local TV station, never got to see her naked. Okay, maybe once or twice, but that was it. And it was well over a year ago.

Snuggled in bed, Viv continued to watch the video. Just. A. Little. More. Prep. For. Tomorrow's. Meeting. *Oh God.* She was actually pacing her thoughts to Jarod's thrusts. This was getting out of hand.

Suddenly, Jarod stopped all motion and began talking. But this wasn't idle chitchat. Even if she couldn't make out the words, she could tell it was intense and demanding, and apparently so hot it made the woman's eyes roll back in her head. Viv messed with the volume, straining to hear him, to no avail.

What the hell did he say?

She couldn't read Jarod's lips because they were fastened on Video Girl's ear, and she couldn't sweeten the audio without the studio equipment they had at the office. It was driving Viv crazy. Not that it really mattered for her work. It was her own curiosity making her mad. His words, and the effect they had on his woman. *Holy shit.*

Seconds later, they both slumped against the wall, and Viv's chest deflated like a popped balloon. If it were possible, she'd say she just had a vicarious orgasm. Though hers had none of the relief, so she went to the kitchen and snagged the last of the leftover chocolate cake to find her happy place.

Back in bed with her heaping plate, she made it to the last scene in the footage. Jarod pulled up his pants and rubbed the scruff on his chin, looking perfectly sated. Video Girl was not as composed. She was a messy puddle of afterglow, so Jarod helped dress her. It was odd, and also strangely sweet.

Viv wolfed down the remaining morsels of her dessert, relieved the video was finally over. Then she put it out of her mind for the next few hours while she worked. She read about Jarod Cage's racing history and his personal life. And that's when she found another potential crisis to deal with—his engagement to a Gina McKnight, a motocross reporter for ESPN. The article said the two were on the rocks, but still...*what a dumbass.* Yes, his relationship status would definitely have to be addressed.

She continued brainstorming ideas and polishing her presentation until she was confident she had a strategy in place to solve the Cage crisis. At two in the morning, she shut everything down, closed her eyes, and let the exhaustion take her under. Not surprisingly, it didn't last. Viv never slept well the night before a client meeting, so she spent the next six hours tossing and turning, dozing in and out. Only this time it wasn't the stress of the presentation messing with her shut-eye. It was the image of Jarod Cage playing on the screen behind her eyelids and the sounds of his demands vibrating in her ears.

• • •

Viv moved into downward facing dog for the third time in her morning yoga class, desperate for a pair of fresh panties.

Unable to banish the thoughts of Mr. Sex on Wheels and that damn video from the night before, Viv felt dirty and stupid…but mostly, incredibly horny. She was like a groupie or stalker or something, fixated on a man she couldn't have. It was embarrassing, and completely unlike her.

She tried to burn off the shit-pot of nervous energy simmering under her skin, holding each pose longer than anyone in the class. Her Eagle was something to behold. Still, as she twisted her body into various pretzel-like shapes, all she could focus on was her meeting with the notorious bad boy. In two hours.

Maybe morning yoga wasn't such a good idea.

But Viv Blake wasn't a quitter. She toughed out the session, though she felt none of the relief that she usually did by the time the class said *Namaste*. All of the uneasiness had yet to subside, so she hit the locker room hoping a steaming shower would help.

It didn't.

She dried off and slipped into a slate-gray wrap dress and pale pink Louboutins, and, oh yeah, the ensemble worked its magic—lifting her spirits and her measly five-foot-three height. She actually felt more powerful with the shoe's extra inches. So far, so good.

Her makeup was another story. She was hot and splotchy with bags under her eyes, and the minimal makeup she carried in her bag wasn't cutting it. She'd have to polish up her game face at the office, where she kept the big guns (like heavy-duty concealer, eye brightener, and berry lip stain) for mornings such as this.

Making quick work of her long dark hair, she secured it in a loose bun and headed out to the coffee shop across from the firm, ordering an iced dark roast. She really wasn't a fan, but couldn't take regular coffee in this heat. Connecticut had its steamy moments in the summertime, but the Nutmeg State had nothing on Hotlanta.

Viv placed the cool cup up to her forehead as she walked the last block to her building. The city was sleepy for mid-week—even at Elite. Everyone was already off celebrating the holiday, leaving the sorry saps like her to hold down the fort.

By the time she walked into her office, she was a soggy mess. "Good Lord, what happened to you?" Mel asked, sitting on Viv's desk all cute and fresh-faced. Mel was Viv's best friend at the agency. Actually, it felt like she was her only friend most days.

"The heat happened." Viv dumped her bags and moved her cup to her neck and chest, trying to cool down. "Dry heat, my butt."

"Get over here," Mel said. "Let me fix that rat's nest." Mel went to work on her frizzy hair while Viv filled her in on the strategy she developed for the campaign. She needed a second opinion.

"If I want any chance at New York, I have to nail this thing," she said.

"I know." Mel finished Viv's hair with a generous coating of the hair spray she kept in her purse. "But you shouldn't have to kill yourself to do it. You need to tell Miranda to stick it up her ass."

"Right," she said, admiring Mel's handiwork in her compact mirror.

"I'm serious," Mel continued, swinging her legs as they dangled from the desk. "Or you could tell her to get bent.

You know, whatever. Personalize it as you see fit."

Viv laughed at Mel's suggestion about how to handle their boss. If only it were that easy. "I think about that all the time," Viv admitted. Her lips spread into an evil grin as she imagined the look on Miranda's face if she ever got up the nerve to tell her off.

Priceless.

"I can see that." Mel snickered while her friend indulged in the daydream. "Why Viv Blake, you aren't the model employee that you make yourself out to be. So, once you finish planning our boss's demise, what do you say we go out for mimosas?"

"I wish." Viv took the Cage file out of her bag. "In addition to the Miranda situation, I also have to save a porn star today."

"Aw, your parents must be so proud." Mel inspected her manicured fingernails—always in some shade of pink.

"As they should be," Viv deadpanned.

"Why do you get all the fun assignments?" Mel said before belting out her best porn soundtrack—complete with a *boom chicka bow wow* as she gyrated on an imaginary stripper pole.

Viv could just hug her friend. That girl found the positive in any situation. She was the perfect balm to Viv's nerves.

Despite her occasional crudeness, Melody Sharp was a modern-day Southern belle. A pretty, pretty princess. Colorful preppy dresses, monogrammed Jack Rogers, and never a hair out of place. Her blond curls were always tamed to perfection, contrary to Viv's dark mop. Mel was the only person Viv had connected with since college. Her schedule and frequent moves didn't really allow her to make a life outside of work, so friends were a luxury she usually had to forgo. Until she moved to Atlanta. Not that Mel really gave Viv a choice in the matter. She'd been sitting at her desk the first day she arrived, and had greeted her the same way each morning ever since—with a healthy dose of challenge and cheer. Viv bent her rules for Mel. She made room for her, knowing that when the time came for another move, they'd just shift their daily chatfests from the office to Skype.

Viv stopped Mel's impromptu dirty dancing with a smack to her behind. She feigned disgust, but was grateful Mel was there to lighten the situation. She had everything riding on the Cage case and could use all the support she could get. Plus, Mel always knew how to calm her. "What are you doing in here, anyway? It's a company holiday. Don't you have a picnic to prepare for?"

"What can I say?" Mel smiled. "Your work ethic is rubbing off on me. I also had some things to do before the mini vacay and after your text last night, I had to make sure my girl was prepared. Plus, maybe there's still a chance you can come to the festivities tonight? We can't let the Ice Queen ruin all of our plans."

Yes, Viv was living her own personal version of *The Devil Wears Prada*. Her boss even had the name and personality to match. Except in this case, the Ice Queen wore Lilly Pulitzer, and there was no amazing closet full of free clothes or trips to Paris.

"Too late," Viv said, pulling out her makeup bag. "You know I'll be locked away for the next week working on this."

"You're exhausted, darlin'. She's been working you too hard, and now she's dumping the Jarod Cage case on you? It's bullshit."

Viv nodded, working on her eyes. Just a little more concealer and she'd be good to go.

"I'll make her pay," Viv whispered, getting the strange sensation Miranda had the place bugged. "One way or another, you'll see. She won't know it's coming, and she definitely won't know it's me."

"Well, that seems to defeat the purpose." Mel rolled her eyes. "You need to speak up so she stops taking advantage of you."

"Yeah, I know. But I hate confronting that woman. Sometimes the path of least resistance is best."

Mel's brow settled into a rare serious expression. "I'm still worried about you."

"Don't be." Viv put her makeup away with a wink. "How else am I going to get the director role in New York? I have to pay my dues."

"Okay," Mel said. "Back to business, then. I found some racing pubs to get you started." She handed over a stack of magazines.

"Is this from your personal collection?" Viv glanced at the publications.

"Har har. We had a stack in the library. The media relations department does some work for NASCAR. Now is there anything else I can help you with before you get *Caged*?"

Viv raised a brow. "Is that code for something?"

"No, that's just what the pit lizards call their time with Jarod Cage. *Getting Caged.* Get it?"

"Pit lizards?" she asked. "Do I even want to know what those are?"

"The skanks who try to hook up with the drivers," Mel

said. "NASCAR's answer to groupies."

"Ugh. What have I gotten myself into?" Viv dropped her head into her hands.

"Racing, baby." Mel squealed. "And from the looks of your new client, you could have a whole lot of fun with that."

"Fun?" Viv asked as if she never heard the word before.

"Yes." Mel shook her head. "Remember fun? Laugh. Flirt a little. Let him take you for a ride, if you know what I mean."

"Gross."

"I'm serious. You're overworked and underpaid. What's the point of all of this if you can't enjoy yourself once in a while?"

"You're one to talk, you know?"

"What do you mean?" Mel asked. "I go out constantly."

"Sure, but when was the last time you really got excited about someone?"

"My tastes are particular, that's all." She shrugged. "I'm not going to waste my time unless it's the real deal. I'll know when I know. But we're talking about you. It's 2015, Vivi—live a little. Let go for once in your life."

Viv rolled her eyes.

"Gah, you're hopeless," Mel said, bouncing toward the door. "Well, I'll be around if you need my racing expertise, or if any more of those fun little videos pop up."

"Thanks for the generous offer, but I'll be fine. You can run along now. Go to your picnic and leave the heavy lifting to me."

Mel flipped her off, but Viv knew she didn't take her insult seriously. Mel didn't get whipped up about work like she did. She always said she wasn't the long-term career type, and that was a shame because Melody Sharp was one of the best event planners in Atlanta—whether she knew it or not. But the way Miranda was always pushing her friend, Viv was afraid it was only a matter of time before Mel left Elite and let her parents marry her off to some boring Southern gentleman.

Viv shut her office door so she could do a final run-through of her presentation without any disturbances—though she was keeping the theatrics to a minimum with this one. Most of her clients didn't appreciate a big to-do. Of course the agents and managers did, but the ticket to winning business with men like Jarod Cage was to make him feel at home. She needed to convince him that he needed her, that she was the best person for the job.

That's what Elite Public Relations was all about—being the best in the business. Spit and shine. They made problems go away, threw fabulous parties, and brought in loads of the green stuff. By the time Elite's team was done with their clients, their mamas didn't even recognize them. And that's just how they liked it. Even more than that, Viv wanted to win. She also wanted her clients to win. She expected nothing less, inevitable for someone raised by an overachiever like her father, Alan Blake, Esq.

So that's exactly what she planned to do: win. No matter what it took.

After going through the last of the slides, Viv felt the need to vent and work out the last of her jitters, so she made a quick call to her mother while flipping through the racing trade rags.

Her parents still lived in Connecticut and were counting the minutes until she came home—especially her mother, who made the family her life's work. Though she'd never admit it, Corrine Blake hoped Viv would follow in her footsteps, get her Mrs. degree from a good school, and start popping out babies. Viv had other plans. Slowly, her mother got on board. With each passing year, Corrine grew more supportive of Viv's choices. She even seemed envious at times, wanting to hear all the juicy details. Of course, her father thought her job was nothing more than planning parties and going to charity events. Still, she was convinced that once she landed in New York, he'd finally respect her career path.

"Hey, Mom," Viv said when she picked up on the first ring. Her mother always picked up on the first ring.

"Honey," her mom sang. "Getting ready for the big picnic?"

"No." Viv pouted, spinning in her chair to look out the window. Talking to her mom always made her feel like she was five years old again.

"Why not?" she asked.

"I have an emergency situation with a client." Her cheeks warmed as an image of a half-naked Jarod Cage popped into her head.

"Sounds interesting, do tell."

Oh, you have no idea. "I can't give specifics, but I will tell you that I'm entering the world of car racing. NASCAR, for crying out loud. Ugh."

"And?" her mom asked, not getting the joke—which is exactly what it felt like to Viv. A freaking joke.

"I said NASCAR, Mom." She was tempted to throw in a *duh* at the end of her sentence, but thought better of it.

"I'm not sure I see the problem, hon," Corrine said in that soothing way of hers. "That sport is becoming pretty big—even up here. There are a few guys at Dad's firm who go to Daytona every year, if you can believe it."

"I can't. It's just too weird—and kind of redneck, don't you think? All those motorheads talking about how big their engines are."

"Viv, don't be so crass."

"Sorry, but I don't get it. Driving in circles to see which car can go the fastest?"

"I think there might be more to it than that." Her mom chuckled. "I'm sure there's plenty of strategy and skill involved, you just have to read up on it. It sounds pretty interesting to me."

"Read up on it, *pffft*," Viv said, feeling particularly snarky. "I'm not sure you need to be literate to race cars." She rocked in her chair again.

And that's when she spotted him in the periphery. In her office. Mr. Sex on Wheels in the flesh.

Mouthwatering flesh.

She'd recognize him anywhere—especially after watching his performance for hours last night. Now here he was leaning against the wall, watching her. Listening…

"Fuck it all to hell," Viv muttered.

"Well, you sure are in a foul mood." Corrine continued their conversation, oblivious to the fact that Viv was dying a slow death. "You must be tired, because I know I raised you better than this. Is Miranda working you too hard again?"

"Mom," she said, not taking her eyes off Jarod's—whose glare was burning right through her. "I need to go. I'll call you later."

"But honey—"

Click.

This was not happening.

To say Jarod Cage was gorgeous would be like saying chocolate is edible. Understatement times infinity. She knew he was hot. Everyone did. But seeing him in person, just a few feet from where she sat, was an amazing sight. Viv paged through the thesaurus in her head and couldn't find a word to accurately describe the man.

The scruff he sported in the video had grown, just slightly, over the past thirty-six hours. Oh yeah, she had memorized the timeline of events. His thick sandy hair stuck up all over the place, possibly because he hadn't combed it since the mystery sex tape woman had her hands tangled in it. Though she didn't want to think about *that.*

Typically Viv liked her men a little more buttoned up, but Jarod's unkempt look was balanced by a crisp tailored shirt and dress pants. Yet when his sleepy blue eyes narrowed in on her, *holy crap*. No wonder he had sex in bathroom stalls. It was probably the woman's idea. He was a spectacular specimen of a man.

"I'm sorry," Viv said to him, playing dumb. Not a hard task at the moment with her lust-filled brain. "May I help you with something?"

PR Rule Number 6: Never let them see you sweat.

"After hearing that conversation," he began, his voice low and rough, "I'm not so sure."

Chapter Two

When it rains, it fucking pours.

That was Jarod Cage's first thought as he eavesdropped on the woman who was supposed to be saving his career. He wanted to check her out before he was on the spot with a bunch of suits in some conference room. He was glad he did, and not at all surprised by what he heard. This was just how things went for him—out of the frying pan, into the fire. Insert any other fucking cliché that applied. He was in the biggest jam of his career and he was supposed to put his life in *her* hands? This tiny brunette pixie who was wound so tight she probably needed a bar fuck more than he did? Not to mention that she believed his profession was run by a clan of redneck morons.

Hell. No.

She stood and rounded her desk. Damn, the hits just kept on coming. He was lost for a moment, taking in the sight of the latest addition to his payroll, and completely enthralled by way she pulled herself together, the unmistakable look of determination in her wary brown eyes, her rigid posture. He could take notes on that recovery. Yet for some reason, all it did was make him want to unravel her. He immediately homed in on the tie that held her dress together—the only thing standing between him and all that smooth, creamy skin. A tie that could so easily come undone. Jarod took a deep, fortifying breath and slowly dropped his eyes to the floor, pushing away the unwanted thoughts. Until his gaze tripped over the mile-high shoes. His jaw clenched in response.

He was going to kill his manager. Henry warned him last night that his new PR rep was a young woman. But he didn't tell him she was single—he hated the fact that he had already looked at her left hand—or that she was a Yankee. Henry also failed to mention the state of this young woman's body, the texture of her hair, and the suppleness of her lips. In fact, the old man had been acting a little strange about the whole thing. Not that Jarod could blame him. The situation was more than awkward for everyone.

"Ah, you must be Jarod Cage," the Yank said with a grin, slapping a hand to her head as if she didn't know.

Nice try, baby, but your innocent act isn't going to work on me.

Still, the way she said his name did things to his insides—and one special part on the outside—that he couldn't ignore.

"Number nine Toyota," she continued. "Your car, that is. I've been watching some of the racing footage, the big races, and I was impressed. You're having a spectacular year. Professionally, anyway. Your personal life, however, needs some immediate attention."

Did she just insult me for the second time in less than five minutes?

Jarod stilled as the jitterbug went on listing his stats—as well as her unwelcome opinions. No *how was your trip to Atlanta?* No *tell me about yourself.* Absolutely no bedside manner with this one. His gran would've said she was as cold as a banker's heart. What was it about Northerners that made them this way? Always down to business—so impersonal and high-strung.

She took a wobbly step closer, smoothing her dress before extending a hand. *Hmm, now that was interesting.* She was nervous. Or was it the high-rise shoes? Maybe she was just suffering the effects from the monster-sized coffee she had sitting on her desk. The woman talked a mile a minute. Though Jarod preferred to think *he* was the reason her panties were in such a bunch. She should be scared. His first impression of Elite wasn't exactly a good one.

"And you're Viv Blake," he said, taking her fragile, impossibly soft hand in his rough grip. That was a goddamn error in judgment on his part. Touching this woman was not a smart move. Of course she pulled it away almost as quickly as she offered it.

"Vivian," she corrected, squaring her shoulders.

Touché.

She was going to keep it all business. Good for her. Too bad he knew it was an act. On his hunt for her office, Jarod ran into at least three people in the hallway who referred to her as Viv, not to mention the nameplate outside her door.

"Excuse me," he said, trying to figure out her angle. "Let's try that again." His eyes narrowed, taking in her rather boring work space. There were no degrees or awards on display, which told him she was confident in her work, not defensive. But that wasn't all that was missing. There were no personal photos, no knickknacks on the window ledge, no flowers or girlie things. This could just have easily been a man's office—well, except for the unmistakable feminine scent filling his head with salacious thoughts.

Why did he always want what was bad for him?

If there was trouble within a hundred-mile radius, he'd find it. And the way she was looking at him now, as if *he* was infringing on her precious time? It intrigued him more than it aggravated him.

He needed serious help. "You must be *Vivian* Blake," he said, bringing his focus back to the day ahead. He was making too much out of this woman.

"I am," she said as she leaned against her desk, looking him straight in the eyes. "But," she added, "I'm afraid I wasn't expecting you for another thirty minutes or so."

"So it would seem," he said, holding her gaze. Man, he liked tough women. Hard not to when he was raised by two of them—his mother and older sister. But he didn't come across many in his line of work. Women hadn't yet broken through the glass ceiling in racing, so the majority of ladies that he spent time with were either trophy candy or fans trying to get into his pants.

Ms. Vivian Blake was a welcome challenge. She was also the first to break eye contact as she grabbed a file off her desk. He chuckled to himself, considering it a win in his column.

"No worries," she said. "The more time we have together, the better." She paged through the papers that he was sure covered all the details of the illicit behavior that had brought him to Elite. He should be embarrassed, yet he couldn't seem to drum up the energy to care. He'd grown accustomed to the scandals he fell into on a regular basis, so not much fazed him these days.

"See something you like in there?" he asked. Yes, it was a dick thing to say, but for some reason, he wanted to get a rise out of her.

"Not really." Her lips pulled together in a straight line.

Liar.

"Tell me," she continued, "have you said anything to anyone about this?"

"Not exactly my proudest moment," he said. "I'm not running around talking it up, if that's what you're asking."

"No text messages or calls or posts on social media?" she asked, once again looking down at the file.

"Nope. After my manager showed me the footage of my naked ass on a website, I basically shut everything down. I haven't answered my phone since it happened."

"Good, that's very good news." She cleared her throat and looked up, though her eyes decided to take a lazy detour over one particular area of his body before her head jerked upright.

Wait, did she just check out my junk?

Instinctually, Jarod's heart kicked into high gear, and his mouth went dry. He watched her in wonder, this Patron Saint of Naughty Celebrities, who was giving so many mixed signals it was hard to think straight.

Well hell, my day may just be turning a corner.

He hadn't forgiven her for the redneck gibes or trashing his sport, but her perusal of his pants certainly changed the game.

He searched his brain for a pithy comeback, but he was

far too distracted by the gentle bounce of her breasts as she shifted her feet. It was a move that made his cock twitch. If he didn't know better, he'd swear something in the air just crackled.

Or he might just be losing his mind. He was tired, irritable, and now thanks to *Vivian*, uncomfortably aroused as well. It had been a long day already, driving nearly three hours to Atlanta from his home in Cotton Creek, South Carolina. Even longer for his manager, Henry, coming in from Charlotte.

That's where the entire mess began. Goddamn Charlotte, North Carolina. The fucking place was crawling with people who wanted to destroy him. Or put him in his place, which happened to be dead last in the heap. But they hadn't succeeded yet, and he planned to keep it that way.

It was hard to believe it wasn't even two days ago. After a successful race weekend at the Charlotte Motor Speedway, Jarod decided to hang in town and relax for a night. A nice steak dinner at Rusty's and drinks with the guys at a local bar to celebrate the win. He would crash in the room Henry set up for him when he bought the place. It was an apartment, really. Henry, along with Jarod's crew and the other 90 percent of the NASCAR community, lived in Charlotte and provided a home base for the team.

"So your team came in from Charlotte this morning?" Vivian asked, finally making an effort at small talk.

"The team did," he said. "But I live a few hours away from them, so I came out on my own."

"Oh," she said. "That must be hard for"—she seemed to be searching for a word—"business."

"We make it work," he said, irritated, feeling as if he was

being mocked. So much for turning the corner.

Truthfully, living so far away from the guys *was* hard on business. When it was necessary, Jarod stayed with Henry. But most of the time they conducted business with calls and virtual conferences. Jarod often felt guilty being away from his crew so much. Hence his decision to hang out with the guys, and stay at Henry's place, after the weekend race.

Big fucking mistake that was.

Actually, everything was going fine until he ran into his old *friend,* Candace. That girl could tempt a preacher on Sunday. And Jarod Cage was no preacher. So after his little reunion in the bar bathroom, the team had another drink, and then Henry drove him back to his place. No harm, no foul.

A few hours later? Henry was busting down the guest room door to show Jarod the result of his indiscretions.

It was not his best moment. Sadly, it wasn't his worst, either.

He spent the day working with Henry. They held calls with the lawyers, the owners, and even the sponsors. It was a brutal, demeaning day. Anytime the sponsors stuck their noses in his business, the outcome wasn't good.

Henry was the only person holding him together. "We've been in messes before and we've managed to get out of 'em," Henry had assured him. "Just let me handle it, J-boy. Let me handle it."

Of course by that point, Jarod had already worked himself into a state. So he went a few more rounds with his manager, for no reason other than he was pissed with himself. He yelled and threw a few things around before he was finally resigned to let the people who worked for him do their jobs.

The result? Hiring a PR firm to help repair his image. It was a demand that came from on high. And if the Atlanta spin doctors couldn't fix it, his sponsor would pull out, leaving him without a car, pit crew, or money. Not to mention zero chance of qualifying for the Chase—the last run to win NASCARs biggest honor, the Sprint Cup. In racing, you worked for your sponsor, plain and simple.

So here he was in Atlanta, of all places, doing penance for his sins.

Viv fiddled with her pen, clicking it over and over again, while her eyes burned into the door as if it could help her. "Here." Vivian leaned over her desk and picked up more papers. "Let me get you set up in the conference room and I'll come back for my computer."

"That's all right," Jarod said, not letting on that he was about as far as you could be from all right.

How the hell was he going to be able to do this with all the depraved thoughts running through his mind? Especially once he had an unobstructed view of that sweet ass. His gaze traveled farther down her legs and he felt the zipper in his pants strain.

Pull it together, Cage.

Christ, this was what the bar fuck was supposed to take care of. He couldn't be dealing with his hormones during the racing season. He thought one good lay would set him right, at least for a few weeks. But that wasn't going to hold him. Not when he was supposed to be working with a woman whose body screamed sex.

He worked desperately to keep his shit together and took a seat in one of Viv's guest chairs. "I'll just relax for a moment while you gather your things."

"Ah—" Viv said, her voice shaking.

Good. He wanted her as unbalanced as he felt. "Take your time."

"O-okay," she said. "I won't take long."

She rummaged through her desk for all of her materials while Jarod snatched a racing magazine from the coffee table. He chuckled to himself. It was time to cool things off a bit.

"Hmm," he said. "Sure wish I could read this here periodical, but I guess I'll just look at the purdy pictures."

Viv glanced back at him, her eyebrows knit together. Still, she didn't say a word.

"Ma'am." He pointed to a page inside *Racing Week*. "Can you tell me what this word means?"

There. That was much better. Asshole on offense was much better than dumbass on defense. He could deal with her anger; what he couldn't deal with was silence…or her close proximity.

"Mr. Cage—" Viv began.

"It's Jarod," he said.

"I know what you heard earlier sounded pretty bad, but I was just goofing around. With my mother. On a personal call."

"Mmm-hmm."

"And you came in unannounced," Viv accused.

"True." He gave her a wicked look, unable to control the next words out of his mouth. "But in my defense, I always come unannounced."

It was her fault; she threw him a softball.

Viv's hands stopped rummaging. It looked like her heart

may have stopped beating as well. Her face flashed various shades of red. Oh, this was fantastic. Now time to go for the kill.

"It's more exciting that way, don't you think?"

Viv's teeth dug into her bottom lip so hard, he was sure it'd leave a mark. But he had to hand it to her, she quickly shook it off and focused back on the matter at hand.

That seemed to make him want her all the more—*want* her or want to *fire* her, he hadn't made up his mind yet.

"Look, Mr. Cage," she began.

"Jarod."

"Okay, look, Jarod," she said, her voice still unsteady. "I'm very good at what I do. Very good. Please don't hold those snarky comments against me. Please stay for the presentation before you write me off."

She walked around the desk toward the door, not meeting his eyes. That damn Yank thought he'd follow her. Well, she was in for a surprise. She wasn't getting off that easy. Not by a long shot.

Before Viv could get her hand on the doorknob, Jarod's arm struck like a python, wrapping around her waist to hold her still. The connection sent a jolt riding through him that made his scalp tingle and cock ache. Slowly, carefully, he walked her backward to the chair. She didn't question the move; her body simply went along with his wishes.

He caught her sweet scent that reminded him of his gran's garden of wildflowers, and felt the slightest tremble where his arm held her. He tried to speak, but his throat went as dry as a dirt track after a long race, sending a clear message to his brain: *do not touch this woman.* For once, he tried to listen and released her, motioning to the chair so she'd take a seat.

"I'm not listening to anything, or putting myself on display in front of a dozen strangers, until you tell me why I should give you another second of my time after what you said."

"Because we all make mistakes," she told him, this time without the excuses. "And we all deserve a second chance?"

Jarod knew she probably meant that last comment as a statement, rather than a question. For some reason, the way it came out only made her seem more sincere. He truly believed what she had to say. Still, that didn't mean he had to take it easy on her.

He scratched his jaw, making her suffer and wait. It felt like the temperature in the room shot up at least ten degrees. Viv blew the bangs off her forehead, but he still didn't say anything. She leaned over the desk, waiting. All Jarod could think about was how the position offered an amazing view of her tempting cleavage. He admired it with each rise and fall of her chest, and he hated himself for it. How could he be thinking with his dick at a time like this?

"Okay," he finally said, before he could stop himself. He needed to escape this office and get Henry's read on the whole thing. His judgment obviously could *not* be trusted at the moment.

"Okay?" she asked, looking hopeful. And annoyingly adorable.

"That's what I said."

"Okay." She finally exhaled. "Why don't you follow me and we can join the others?"

• • •

The two of them met Henry in the hallway, and Vivian led the way to the conference room. Henry looked over at Jarod and shook his head as if he could read his mind. He probably could. Henry had been with him since the beginning, and with Jarod's father even longer than that—Tony Cage, aka the General. Racing was in Jarod's blood. It was the one place he connected with his father, and Henry Hayes, top crew chief in NASCAR, was the best gift Jarod's dad ever gave him.

Once Jarod started racing, Tony Cage sent his crew chief to work for his only son's organization. It wasn't a good career move for Henry, but he never balked. Instead, he focused all his efforts on making Jarod the best driver he could. He managed everything for the younger Cage. He was always present, even when Jarod's own father wasn't.

Henry grimaced as they walked down the hall. Deep shadows under his eyes made him look much older than his fifty-five years.

"Okay there, old man?" Jarod, said under his breath.

"I'm just sorry for you, J," Henry said, but it seemed more than that. He wasn't looking so hot. Jarod would need to find a way to give him some time off. Guilt swirled deep in the pit of his gut. He'd let him down so many times, and he knew that managing the fallen golden boy of racing had to be the worst of all jobs. Right up there with the guys in charge of the sewage lines for all the motor coaches that sat in the infield during the races. Yet Henry always had his back.

Even before the sex tape, Jarod didn't exactly have the best reputation. But in his defense, it wasn't easy to look good standing next to Tony Cage. His father was the pillar of the racing world. Everything NASCAR stood for.

Jarod could never measure up. Truthfully, he never wanted to. During his childhood, he watched his father kowtow to the owners, perform for the press, and shell out every last bit of personal time he had to the fans. Jarod wasn't cut out for that life. So he steered clear of all of it, and that put a target on his back.

After Tony Cage was killed during the Sprint Cup Contender Round, the media took it easy on Jarod. Gave him a free pass. But it expired after a year, and then things went back to normal. Tony was declared a saint, and his son was marked a sinner.

It wasn't all that inaccurate. But Henry was right, this wasn't the first time they went through the damn fire drill. And they'd come out of it before without getting burned. Unfortunately, this situation was different. They had no choice in the matter, so he'd go along with this dog and pony show—even if he thought it was another disaster waiting to happen.

Miranda already had the crisis team assembled on one side of the table in the conference room when they arrived. Apparently Viv was the only person who didn't get the memo that they were coming in early, which Jarod found odd considering she'd be his primary contact.

Something didn't smell right.

Jarod took the open seat that his *people* left for him in the middle of the table. He had three other men with him in addition to Henry, but it wasn't Jarod's idea. He fucking hated traveling with an entourage; it made him feel like a world-class asshole.

All the eyes in the room moved toward him. It was a

little uncomfortable, but Jarod had grown accustomed to strangers being involved in every aspect of his life. He'd just do what he always did. Listen to the experts, and then make his own decisions. This time, though, he had no intention of apologizing. Pretty ridiculous considering he just got caught with his pants down—literally—and was at risk of losing millions of dollars. Still, though his behavior may have been a little sketchy, he was the real victim. *He* was the person being wronged, and if these experts didn't get that, they could all go to hell.

Of course, as he went over those last thoughts, he realized he *wasn't* the only person wronged that night.

Shit, I am such an asshole.

Why'd it take him so long to think of someone other than himself? There was also Candace, and he could only imagine the backlash she was dealing with after this latest scandal. He'd be sure to call her after the meeting. She was a good girl and shouldn't have to suffer because of his crazy life. Right now, however, it was time to take care of the business at hand.

After Jarod was settled, Miranda made the introductions. She was also a beautiful woman, in a high-maintenance kind of way. She reeked of money, and power, and maybe even a dash of corruption. Jarod could easily read people. Shit knows, he'd had enough practice. You didn't get to where Miranda was by taking the high road, and he had the feeling she always got what she wanted. Interesting.

Miranda went around the room with the pleasantries, but paused when she reached Viv, like she was implying something. Jarod took it all in.

"And I see you've already met Viv," she said.

"Yes, I have," Jarod responded, leaning away from the table and taking up more space than he could possibly need. It was all part of the game. "I had to check out Ms. Blake myself before we got this show on the road. No sense in wasting anyone's time—or what little money I may have left—if she doesn't have the goods, right?"

"And does she?" Miranda asked in her own commanding voice. "Have the goods, that is?"

Jarod looked over to see Viv holding her breath, as if expecting him to throw her under the bus. *Not just yet,* he thought.

"We'll see, Miranda," Jarod said, casually using her name to take back control.

"Wonderful." She shared a pirate smile. "Shall we begin then?"

"Let's." Jarod returned her fake grin with one of his own.

"Viv," Miranda said. "Why don't you bring Mr. Cage's team up to speed?"

Quickly loading her presentation, Viv hooked up the projector and went over the introductory slides. Jarod knew this was the warm-up before getting personal.

"So." Viv took a deep breath, before diving in. "I've gone over the tape, and we had our tech team take care of any leftover remnants hiding out online."

Or maybe not.

"Our legal team should've done that already," Henry said.

"Yes," Viv agreed. "They did a great job, but you'd be amazed how many sites find ways to slink around the system. Like I said, it wasn't the entire video, but pieces of it here and there. For the most part, it's disappeared from cyberspace. But we can't ignore the damage that's already been done. So we need to get in front of it."

"What do you mean, 'get in front of it'?" Jarod asked, not at all happy with the sound of that.

"We need to hold a press conference to address the situation," Viv told him.

"No," Jarod said immediately, shaking his head.

"I'm sorry, Mr. Cage. What do you mean *no*?"

"It's *Jarod*, and I mean *no*. If I wanted people poking around in my business, I would live in Charlotte with all the other wheelmen. I'm not giving in to them."

"Wheelmen?" Viv asked.

"Drivers," he snapped before turning to his manger. Christ, she had no clue about the world he lived in. How could she possibly help him?

Henry swallowed and placed his hand on Jarod's arm, silently telling him they needed a quick powwow.

"Vivian, Miranda, could you give us a minute?" Jarod asked.

"Sure," Miranda said, escorting the Elite team out. "Take all the time you need."

Jarod leveled a look at his manager, and when the door shut, he released holy hell.

Chapter Three

"You better not blow this one for us, Viv," Miranda said as the team reconvened in the employee lounge. She punched the keys on her cell phone, while Fredrick the Weasel handed her another file. Miranda's right-hand man was her nemesis. Also in the executive program, but at least a year behind Viv, he was an ass-kisser and basically made her work life hell whenever he got the chance.

"I won't, Miranda," she said, racking her mind for a way to save this client. "I promise."

"To be sure," she said, looking bored as usual. "Let me dangle a carrot. Get Jarod Cage to the Chase, with his reputation and sponsors intact, and you'll be next in line for the New York position."

"But Miranda," Fredrick interjected. "I thought— "

Miranda didn't even look his way when she took the call coming in on her cell. Viv gave her a mental high-five for that move. But even in her own imagination, Miranda left her hanging.

"Shut it, Fred," Viv said. "By the way, I know it was you who conveniently forgot to tell me Cage was coming in early."

"Oops," he said, cocking his head in challenge.

She was ready to hang him by his bow tie before Miranda interrupted.

Covering the phone, their fearful leader added, "And Viv, that means you have two months to get the job done. If not, you're mine for another year."

Frederick choked down his pleasure at this development, while Viv choked down her breakfast. This was an impossible situation.

She now had a (potential) client who lived in a world she knew nothing about. A client so insanely hot she could hardly form a sentence whenever he was near. A client who already hated her, and now she had sixty days to save his career and help him win a metal cup. Or she'd have to put up with the Ice Queen for another year—the woman who would trample a class of preschoolers to get out of a burning building, or sell her mother's soul to ink a big deal.

She was *so* screwed.

The group spread out, taking calls and typing texts, waiting for the Cage crew to reemerge. Viv took post just outside the conference room door, listening to Jarod's booming voice.

"Jesus, Henry," Jarod yelled. "I thought you said this firm is the best?"

"They are, Jarod. They come highly recommended."

"Well, the lead on the account doesn't know a fucking thing about racing."

"But," Henry said, "she knows a helluva lot about repairing reputations."

Viv gave Henry a mental high-five. Unlike Miranda, he was kind enough to reciprocate. The voices suddenly went quiet and Viv could no longer hear what was going on, so she leaned in. The movement caught Jarod's eye.

Busted.

The next moment, the door opened and Jarod leaned against the doorway. "Can we just get right to the point here?"

"Yes," she said, happy Miranda wasn't in close proximity to hear the tongue lashing.

"Setting what happened this morning aside, it's very clear you're not a NASCAR gal," he said. "So tell me, why should I hire you?"

"I'm not a NASCAR *gal,*" she said, speaking as quietly as she could to avoid alerting her boss. "But I am a PR gal, and a damn good one. I specialize in crisis communications, and all my clients happen to be in the entertainment industry. I can tell you from experience that the only way to be successful in crisis communications is to *communicate* in a crisis. Bottom line. We need to have that press conference. We have to, Jarod. And this is why you should hire me, because I know what I'm doing, and I'm not afraid to tell you what I really think."

"Well, I'm in the business of racing, Viv," he said with dancing eyes. "And the first rule in racing is never let them catch you."

"I understand that. I do. But it looks like you've been caught this time, and there's no easy way out of it. If you want to save your career, you need to listen to me. Please, let me help you."

Jarod held up a finger, pulling Henry back inside the room.

She watched from the window. It felt like they were in there for an eternity. Jarod was a live wire, bouncing off the walls, tearing his fingers through his hair, pounding on the table. His movements were big and bold, while Henry moved in a slow, patient, almost methodical way. She watched as he eased Jarod down, one step at a time. She could learn something from him.

When Jarod finally came out, he gave her a brisk nod. "Okay," he said. "Let's get this over with as fast and painlessly as possible."

She delivered on her client's first request immediately by convincing Miranda to let her finish up with Jarod—alone. She knew he wasn't going to tell her what she needed to know in a big group like that, and if this was going to work, she had to smooth things over with him and start building trust.

"Okay," Miranda said, pulling her into a corner as the group dispersed. "But use your instincts on this one. Don't let me down."

"I won't," she said, though she had no idea what her boss was talking about.

"We'll discuss your progress at the end of the day," she added, before clicking her way down the hall to chat with Jarod's manager.

Strange, he didn't seem high enough in the ranks to command Miranda's time. She must really want to make them happy.

Viv led Jarod back to her office, and the rest of the team

packed up for the day. She was happy about that. No sense ruining everyone's holiday.

"Sweet tea?" she offered him once they were in the comfort of her own space.

"No, thank you," he said politely.

Uh-oh. Maybe some small talk will warm him up.

"It's weird," Viv began, gesturing to him to take a seat. She had to find a way to break his chilly demeanor. "In any other sport, this *situation* wouldn't be that big of a deal. But because you rely so heavily on your sponsors, they have a lot more power over you. It must be tough."

"Not really," Jarod said, not at all interested in the conversation.

"Fair enough." Viv sat in the chair across from his and set up her laptop on the end of the coffee table. She would have to change her strategy quickly, so she wouldn't bruise his fragile ego. *Fucking celebrities.* "I'm sure you hold the cards. I mean, what happens in the pit stays in the pit, right?"

"Did you get that from one of your magazines?" he asked, pointing to the pile of *NASCAR Illustrated, Circle Track,* and *Motor Sport.*

"Hey, I take research very seriously. I just need a little time and I'll be up to speed on all of it. But right now, it'd help if you could shed some light on a few things for me."

"Such as?"

He wasn't going to make this easy.

"Well, how do all the other drivers avoid these mishaps? There's very little scandal in NASCAR, so why is this happening to you?"

"I think it's pretty obvious from the video, don't you?" he asked, and Viv couldn't stop the scenes that flashed in her brain again.

"Okay, these smart-ass answers aren't going to help anyone," she said, unable to hold back. "And I have to say I really don't understand why you aren't taking any of this seriously."

"I take it very seriously, Viv. This is my life, so you'll have to excuse me if I'm not ready to share my feelings with somebody who not only doesn't *get* my life, she mocks it."

She closed her eyes, feeling like the world's biggest bitch.

"I'm sorry about that," she said one final time. "It won't happen again, I assure you. I really want to understand how all this works."

"Really?" he asked, and Viv could almost feel his vulnerability. Was there some sweetness under the bad-boy demeanor?

"Please," she said. "I honestly want to know."

"Well," he said. "First of all, the image of racing? The family values and all that shit is completely legit. This sport—the owners, the fans, the sponsors—simply won't tolerate assholes. And they won't allow their image to be tainted by scandal."

"And how do you feel about that?" Viv asked.

"Well, I don't tolerate assholes either, so I guess we have that in common," Jarod said jokingly, but she thought there just might be more to his words.

He tipped his head to meet her eyes. "What?" he asked.

"Nothing," she said. "You're just not what I expected."

"I get that a lot." He grinned then, and Viv's body buzzed. All from a little smile. Yes, Jarod Cage was absolutely electric, and despite her best effort to be professional, she was drawn to him.

"Well, let's get you out of this mess then. Shall we?"

"I'd like nothing better."

"Since you brought up family values, we need to talk about your fiancée, Gina McKnight, and how she's feeling after the video went public." Viv clicked her mouse over her notes. It was one of the more disturbing details she uncovered during her research. Not unusual—most of these guys were cheaters—but still disappointing. Not that it should matter to her one way or another. "I haven't seen anything from her in the press yet, but I'm sure it's only a matter of time. What's going on there?"

"I don't have a fiancée," Jarod answered simply.

"Yes, I'm sure, in light of everything that's happened—"

"No," he interrupted. "That much was true even before the video was released."

And here come the lies. Viv checked her imaginary watch. *Right on time.*

"Well, it's neither here nor there." She brushed it off, trying to move on. She was used to guys like Jarod lying to her—even in the middle of a crisis.

"Actually, I think it is both here and there." Jarod raised his voice. "I wouldn't have done *that* if I were engaged."

"Okay, tell me." She let out a painful sigh. "How long has the engagement been off?"

"It was never on," he said.

"Are you saying that you were never engaged?" she asked.

"Yes, ma'am."

Hmm. Now we're getting somewhere.

"Then why does everyone think you are?"

"Because that's what my ex told them," he said. "She wants to be with a driver. Period. And she will work any angle she can to land one."

"Why don't you set the press straight?" she asked, getting a little upset on his behalf.

"They don't care about the truth," Jarod said. "They never came to me to verify anything. And I'm not going to seek out the media. I don't care what they say about me."

"Well, it matters now. Wouldn't you say?"

Jarod shrugged, so she kept on task. "Okay, the fact that you aren't engaged—and weren't when the tape was made—is definitely something we can use. Still, the images on that video. Well, I see a lot of it in this line of work and *I* can't get it out of my head."

"Is that so?" He grinned.

"Okay, now this is something else we need to work on," she said in frustration.

"What?" he asked, feigning innocence.

"This bad-boy image you have going on here."

"It's not an image," he said.

"Regardless. If you want me to help you, you're going to have to listen to me. You need to be on the straight and narrow, mister. I'm serious. No sex in bathrooms. No sex—period. At least for the time being. You need to be in early, spend your nights at home, and we need to create an approved list of all your *acquaintances*."

Jarod let out a deep belly laugh and slapped the desk. "You want to put me on a curfew and monitor my every move like I'm some pimply teenager?"

"Yes, I do." Viv wasn't going to budge on the demands.

"No way." He crossed his arms, defiant.

"Way." She exaggerated her response to sound like a teenager, just as he did. It made his eyes dance again, and the faintest of smiles had his lips turning up a smidge.

"Okay." He stroked his chin again. "Then if this is going to work, you'll also need to do something for me."

"And what's that?" she asked, knowing she was approaching dangerous territory.

"Have you ever heard of quid pro quo?"

"Gah, don't say that." She shivered. "I *hate* that term. It reminds me of *Silence of the Lambs*. And also my dad's work."

"Your father's a lawyer?"

She nodded.

"Interesting," he said, studying her face. "There is something that gets under your skin, tough girl."

"There's a lot that gets under my skin," she admitted.

"Really, do you still hear the screaming of the lambs, Clarice?" Jarod said, trying for his best Anthony Hopkins.

She had to hand it to him. He was clever and, as Mel predicted, quite fun. Those were good qualities in a client. Now if only she could do something about her body's unrelenting pull toward him. Her yoga instructor would tell her to surrender to the uncomfortable feelings and release them out into the world so she could move on, but that wasn't her style. Her motto had always been: *keep them guessing*.

"Geez, only *you* could make a serial killer sound sexy." The words came out before she realized their implication.

"You think I'm sexy?" he asked in that honey-laced Southern drawl that had become yet another hurdle Viv had to clear while working with this man.

God, yes.

"That's not what I said." She avoided his eyes and his question.

He inched closer and reached out to toy with her

bracelet, reading the inspirational message: *Believe*. Typically Viv didn't do corny, but her mother bought it for her after graduation and it made her feel good every time she wore it.

"A gift from my mom," she said.

"It's sweet." Jarod's knuckles brushed along her arm as he studied the jewelry. It felt as if it was an invitation to something more, and Viv secretly wished for a bar bathroom to materialize.

"Okay, so about the quid pro quo?" Jarod circled back.

"Yeah, about that. You want to watch one of my sex tapes—is that what you're asking?"

"Well, that'd be great, actually. Level footing and all of that, Vivian."

"Sorry pal, you're barking up the wrong tree. I don't have one." It was the truth, and she wondered if that made her seem prudish to a guy like Jarod.

"No boyfriend then?" he asked.

She shook her head, and thought she saw the trace of something resembling relief wash over Jarod's face. Or was that wishful thinking on her behalf?

"Well, you have to give me something," he said.

"Like what?" she asked, caught up in his spell. Dazed. He had such finesse in the art of talking—or was it flirting?—something the men in her past lacked. She was ill-equipped to handle his sweet-talking ways.

He simply raised an eyebrow, and deep down, she wanted to give him anything he asked for. She was tired and stressed to the limit. So was he. Maybe that's why they continued with the juvenile banter.

The scene was becoming more and more surreal. Having Jarod Cage this close in her office was the equivalent of having a porn star in her bedroom. She had seen this man do things that nobody should see. Especially if that person was your client. She considered *giving him something*, the quid pro quo, knowing that's all it was—nothing more, just something to even the playing field. She needed to take action to gain his trust if this was going to work. They were both putting their futures in the other's hands.

Something had to break here, and that something just might be her. It might not be such a bad thing. Once they cleared the air of all the sexual tension, they could get back to work.

Jarod didn't say a word when she pressed him for an answer. But Viv, in her wound-up state, knew just how to shut him up. Act like a man. Take the challenge. She would not lose this project. She'd get Jarod Cage to his little race and secure her position in New York, but first she'd have to tame the beast. Then he'd be out of her system.

PR Rule Number 3: Be proactive.

She could do that. So without giving it a second thought, she went on *instinct*. She stood up, untied her wrap dress, and let it drop to the floor. Yeah, probably not exactly what Miranda meant. It was a good thing she wasn't around to see this.

There. Quick and painless, like he said earlier.

Except it was neither.

"Is this what you had in mind?" she asked, steadying herself. "Your way to even the score between us? Okay, have at it. Take a nice long look."

She pushed her feet into the floor, imagining they were growing roots to anchor her. It's the method her yoga teacher used to help the class with their balance, and she needed all the balance she could get.

Then she stood there on display in her best bra and panty set—the pale lime-green lace demi cup that held her up fabulously, and a pair of booty-hugging panties in the same delicious fabric. They were the undergarments she never had a need for until now, because let's face it, the ensemble was less than comfortable. Still, she thanked the gods she was so well-prepared for this unexpected moment.

It got his attention all right. His mouth dropped open and he froze.

That's right, Cage. My ball. My court.

"My God, what are you trying to do to me?" His voice was raw.

She may have been known for her original tactics with clients, but this was off the charts batshit. Straight up stupid crazy. Something that was becoming even more evident as Sex on Wheels slowly rose and began to close the distance.

He squeezed his eyes shut briefly and released a deep and labored breath, but he didn't stop coming toward her.

Oh no, no, no.

He hesitated for a moment before running a single finger down her arm, not to be overshadowed by her brash move. Goose bumps peppered the skin in Jarod's wake, and she found herself leaning into his touch.

Until the knock on her office door.

Viv nearly jumped out of her skin at the sound. She snagged her dress off the floor and grabbed Jarod by the arm and pulled him into her coat closet.

They made it inside before the next knock.

"Viv," the visitor called from outside.

"Shhh," she whispered to Jarod.

The squeak of the door sounded.

She held her breath, panic coursing through her veins. They held still, neither of them moving. What in the hell was she thinking pulling that crap?

Jesus H., not only was she going to lose out on New York, she was going to be fired from Elite altogether. Rumors would circulate about her slutty stunt and she'd never work again. Viv's temples ached as she envisioned the brutal end of her career.

Or they did, until Jarod exhaled, soft and warm, on the back of her neck.

Her neurosis instantly took a backseat to her libido, and in that moment, she didn't give a rat's ass who might be standing in her office. Her heart beat so fast she could feel it in her toes. It took everything in her power not to jump his bones. She'd never wanted anything more.

A few footsteps echoed in the room, and then nothing. All the while, Jarod was crammed up against her almost-naked body. He used the opportunity to hold her by the hips, telling her exactly who was in charge. Her body was burning up, and the idea of getting caught only added to the thrill.

The door finally shut again.

"Shit," she said, taking her first breath in what felt like an hour. "They're gone."

She turned toward him in the tight space, and may have blacked out for a moment when her breasts made contact with his chest. She expected Jarod to back away, or open the door, but he didn't move a muscle—if you didn't count the one that was currently pushing up against her belly. Viv couldn't help it as her mind rolled back to the infamous video. The thought of him lifting her, pushing into her, saying whatever the hell it was that he said to Video Girl. Of course now, knowing about his acumen in the art of dirty talk, she knew it was something beautifully filthy.

"We can go," she finally said, covering herself with the dress.

"I want nothing more than that," he said. "I wish we could leave, but we can't, not now. Not after I've seen you."

"I gave you your quid pro quo. I saw you in an uncompromising position and you saw me. Now we can put it behind us and get back to work." Viv prayed her words sounded convincing.

"Not quite the same thing," he said. He cracked the closet door open and the soft light flooded in, bringing Jarod's sharp features into focus. His eyes feasted on her body, his hands moved back to her hips to hold her in place, and she was lost again.

"I don't understand," she said in her foggy state.

"I don't either," he said. "I shouldn't want this, but there's something I have to know." His thumbs marked her skin in lazy circles. "Did you watch the entire video?"

"Yes," Viv said, resisting the urge to let her head fall back and succumb to his tortuous touch. "I had to. I needed to know what we were dealing with."

"The way I *fuck* is important to your work?"

Oh God, don't say that word.

Her nipples tightened, threatening to slice right through the pretty lace of her bra. Jarod hissed, yet it was Viv who felt the tug deep in her core.

"I had to be thorough," she defended herself. "I didn't know what else was on the video."

"So you watched it until I came, didn't you?"

It wasn't a question, though Viv still felt obligated to answer. "Yes."

He held her gaze—this insanely beautiful man with his filthy mouth—and consumed her space while she fought for air.

"Yes," he said, nodding as if he reached an important conclusion. "Yes, you did. You watched a very personal moment of mine, Vivian."

Making him use her full name was a mistake. She thought it'd help create distance, but the way it rolled off his tongue only excited her. She tried to follow the conversation, desperately working to ignore the effects of his low raspy voice, his citrus scent, and the way his fingers dug into her soft flesh. She was failing miserably, on the train past crazy, heading toward the stop marked certifiable.

"Well, there you have it," he said.

"Have what?" Viv momentarily surfaced from her pheromone-induced state.

"That's what *I* want," he said. "I can't explain why, but I need the same from you."

Jarod slid her bra straps down her arms, one at a time. His eyes fixed on hers, daring her to object. When she didn't, he used his thumb to trace the outline of each hardened nipple. She gasped and shuddered, latching onto his arms so she wouldn't fall.

"Christ, woman," he groaned, and in the very next instant, he unlatched her bra and was rolling her sensitive peaks in his fingers before the lace hit the closet floor.

This time, Viv couldn't keep her pleasure contained. "Oh God," she moaned.

"I want the chance to see you come," he said softly,

simply, like it was a perfectly reasonable request. "Then we'll be even. Then we can move on."

If he kept this up, she would more than grant his request.

Jarod eased his thumb into Viv's mouth before whispering, "Suck."

She did as he asked and pulled him deep into her mouth, stroking his thumb with her tongue in a not-so-subtle display of her own prowess. His lips opened then, a rough sigh escaping. She knew just how he felt, wanting more, needing it so much it hurt.

Jarod used the moisture from her mouth to torture her nipples, plucking and pinching. The intense contact left her a whimpering mess. Pain, relief, and something chasing ecstasy alerted her pleasure center all at the same time. She couldn't distinguish one feeling from the other, and didn't know whether she should be pleased or pissed.

He didn't ask for permission, didn't warm her up. Rather, he took was he wanted. It was like nothing she'd ever experienced before.

Jarod released his hold on her aching nipples and dropped his head down to place a soothing wet kiss on each. Viv found herself arching into his mouth. Bowing and bending, anything to get closer to him.

He didn't kiss her mouth. Didn't embrace her. Yet he treated her body with such quiet reverence. It was soul-baring and intoxicating, and she never wanted it to end.

Yes, she knew it was purely physical. And no, she didn't do hookups. But Mel was right; it was past time she let herself go. She could do this. More importantly, she wanted to.

"You are sweet as hell," Jarod said in between kisses. "I bet you're sweet everywhere, aren't you?"

Viv wanted to reciprocate. Hell, she wanted to touch him out of her own selfish need for him. But each time she made a move, he locked her hands in one of his. There was no question who was in control.

He ran a calloused palm down her breasts, over her ribs, and across her stomach. The scraping of his rough skin on her smooth flesh woke every sleeping cell in her body and made it hum.

Suddenly, he stopped, resting his forehead on hers, slowing things down. His breathing deep and ragged. Maybe he was reconsidering.

Please, no.

It seemed he was as confused as she was—waging a battle for his own control. Turns out, it didn't matter. Jarod officially waved his white flag of surrender. He moaned, low in his throat, and that python of an arm struck again, leaving no room for doubt as he ripped her panties clear off her body.

It was distasteful, inconsiderate, and so damn hot he was about to have his wish come true in the next ten seconds. Viv was completely bare to him and so close to the edge she could feel it in every fiber of her body. But ending this so fast would be a freaking shame. Everyone knew about Jarod Cage. He was a bad boy. A ladies' man. Actually, a bit of a manwhore. He was also gorgeous, and skilled, and so damn dirty.

When would Viv ever get this kind of chance again?

Jarod moved her legs apart and found her wet and ready for him. Viv abandoned the last shred of pride she had and let him guide and instruct her as he pleased. He ran a long finger down her seam and growled in appreciation. "I want to see," he said, cracking the door open a little further. His thumbs spread her wide for him as he studied the most private part of her. "God, look at you."

She should be concerned about the door. Damn it all, why wasn't she concerned about the door? It was risky and careless, but at this point, she didn't care about anything other than the way Jarod was touching her.

"Now tell me what *you* want," he said. "Please."

"I want—" Viv tried, but stopped when his mouth closed over her nipple again. This time, in a not-so-soothing way. He nipped and sucked, while teasing her with his hand below. She inched her legs apart a little more, needing him deeper. "I want to know what you said to her," Viv finally confessed.

Her head reeled as fantasy and reality converged and collided. His rough consuming touch was a heady aphrodisiac. On steroids. And the way he peeled back her inhibitions, layer by layer, was nothing short of a miracle. It was also fucking fantastic.

"Said to whom?" Jarod asked, slowing his hand, waiting.

"Video Girl," Viv answered.

"Candace?" His hand halted.

"It's good you got her name," Viv said, grinding her hips into his hand, frustrated with the way he was tormenting her.

"I know more than that," he said, holding his fingers so close to her entrance without moving any further. "She's actually a good friend."

"I'm sorry," she said. "I didn't mean to insult you. Or her. I'm just trying to find fault with her to make myself feel better. I know I'm not your typical flavor."

Stop babbling this second, Viv.

"I don't have a flavor, but if I did, you'd definitely be in the mix. But enough of that silliness. I need to know why, of all things, you want to know what we talked about?"

"It's just…she looked so blissed out. So satisfied. I can't help but wonder what you said that made her turn to a pile of mush while you were…"

"Fucking her?" Jarod filled in the blanks.

Viv's insides began to liquefy.

"Yes. Tell me, please."

"You really want to know?" He backed Viv up against the wall of the closet and licked the shell of her ear and then drove two fingers deep inside her. He began pumping relentlessly and Viv almost forgot what she was asking for. "Okay, baby," he muttered. "Okay."

Pressure mounted between her legs, a magnificent ache she hadn't experienced in so long. She began to sway her hips. Rocking into each thrust. She wanted more of him. Craved it. His fingers and mouth and that glorious cock she felt rubbing against her belly earlier.

"I knew there was a prize waiting for me under this dress," Jarod said, continuing to work his skilled fingers. "I love this pussy. Everything about it. The way it looks; the way it feels. Next time, I want a nice long taste. I want you to save it for me. Only me. Will you do that?"

Viv nodded her head, letting his words drive her closer. Damn, she thought she might give Video Girl a run for her money with her reckless abandon. Jarod tripped a switch inside her, and she wasn't sure she'd ever work right again.

Jarod stilled his hand and said, "I want to be able to come here, where you work, and get what's mine. Do you understand?"

His dirty voice wrapped her in a state of pure bliss. Yes, Jarod Cage was that smooth. That good. No wonder he made women come apart in public bathrooms. The man had a way with words. At least those words were no longer a mystery—she was now part of the club.

As she tightened around him, he curled his fingers and the used the heel of his hand to put an insane amount of pressure on her clit. So, so good. She wanted to freeze time, stay in this moment just a little longer.

But she needed more.

She begged and Jarod gave in. His blunt fingers pushed deep inside and pulled out painfully slow, again and again, working her into a frenzy. And just when she thought she couldn't take any more, he drove those fingers into her at such a furious pace, she let go and fell headfirst into the most earth-shattering orgasm of her life. It ripped through her, leaving no part untouched. She opened her mouth and Jarod caught her cries with a demanding kiss.

In. Credible.

She didn't come to immediately after that. She was long gone, suspended in that space between bliss and reality, and unable to make sense of anything that had just transpired. Jarod was all there was—his scent, his massive arms, his warm breath on her neck. She floated back and slumped against this man she hadn't known for more than a few hours, until she could feel her limbs again.

He didn't rush her.

"How was that?" he asked, after recovering her dress from the floor and wrapping it around her protesting body. She was far too sensitive for clothes. Her skin craved the comfort of a hot-blooded man, not the cotton blend she was currently covered in. But she realized that was out of the question.

"I should be asking you the same thing," she said,

tightening the tie on her dress and smoothing down her knotted hair. She knew there was no time to bask in the afterglow, so she ushered them both out of the closet. "That was your quid pro quo. Was it worth it?"

"Oh yeah," Jarod said, his voice doing that low raspy thing she was beginning to love. "It was totally worth it."

I couldn't agree more.

"Happy to hear it." She patted him on the side of his shoulder in the world's most ridiculous gesture of thanks. But really, what was proper etiquette after letting a client finger you in the closet? Oh, she could think of better ways to reciprocate. So, so many ways. And that thought scared the hell out of her.

"That was a onetime thing though," she said, feeling the need to clear the air—for her as well as him. "You know that, right? I really don't even know what came over me. I don't do things like this. Ever."

"Blame it on the heat wave," he said.

"Seriously?" she asked, hopeful. "Is that really a thing?"

"Absolutely," he said, but he wasn't at all convincing.

She wondered if that's the excuse he used with Video Girl. *Shit.* That reminded her…

"Wait, Jarod," she said, remembering his words. "Video Girl worked at the restaurant? That is not good. We're going to have to prepare for the possibility of a lawsuit. Let me call—"

"Hold on there." Jarod stopped her. "Candace doesn't work at Rusty's."

"But just a minute ago you said all that stuff about coming to her work."

"I didn't say those words to her, Vivian. Those were my

words to you. I don't need to use leftovers. Believe me, I have no issue coming up with my own material where you are concerned."

"Oh," she said, at a loss.

Oh, wow.

"But I wanted the complete Video Girl experience," Viv joked, trying to make light of her own experience so he wouldn't know how profoundly he affected her.

"There's still time, baby," he taunted.

"Oh, no, you don't. We're even. You've seen me. I've seen you. And now the monkey is off my back. From this point forward, this relationship is strictly business."

"If you say so." Jarod laughed.

Viv went to open the door. She couldn't get him out of there fast enough. It was a lot to take in for a morning.

He shoved a hand in his pocket in that easy way of his, taking Viv's hint with grace. It disarmed her completely.

How did he do that?

"Well, I better be on my way, then," he said.

"Don't forget, we have the thing tomorrow," she reminded him, trying to keep it as casual as possible. She didn't need him freaking out over a press conference.

"On Uncle Sam's birthday?"

"No rest for the horny," she quipped. "Plus, it's the best day for a press conference. You'll make one news cycle and then you'll be able to put this all behind you. Especially once people see all the good you're doing."

"What do you mean, all the good I'm doing?" he questioned.

"Let's just say, I have a lot of plans for you." She went back to her desk. "See you tomorrow."

Chapter Four

Well, that happened.

Jarod wasted no time jumping in his Tundra for the trip home. He loved to drive his truck, and it usually provided the perfect way to decompress from his exhausting life. Unfortunately, there wasn't a comforting thought in his head at the moment. His mind raced, trying to make sense of what had just happened. And he was not the type of person to second-guess his instincts, especially when it came to women.

Maybe it was time to change that after his back-to-back fuckups.

And for the foreseeable future, things were only going to get worse. In exactly twenty-four hours he would have to spill his guts on television for the world to see.

My poor fucking mother.

That was his most disturbing thought since he first watched the clips of his seedy sex tape after it surfaced on-line. He had cringed, straight-up cringed, at the scene on the monitor—his naked ass proudly featured on page one of some media hack's site. He couldn't make out everything, peeking through the fingers that had covered his eyes.

And now he'd be on display once again, rehashing it all and bringing a brand-new variety of embarrassment to his family.

He may have appeared unaffected while he was at Elite, but that was all an act. He was sick over the whole thing, especially knowing the grief he put his family though. Jarod had no problem taking responsibility for his actions. Bar sex was not a wise move—that much was true. But the question that haunted him was: *why would someone tape it?*

He didn't care what his manager said. He wasn't paranoid. Hopefully now, after this latest blow, Henry would believe there was a conspiracy to get him out of racing.

"Hey, Candy," he said, making the needed call to Candace. "Are you surviving, girl?"

"I'm fine," she said, stiffly, not her usual tone with him. He'd known her forever, and they had a lot of water under the bridge, but this was the worst trouble they'd gotten into by far.

It was true he could never give her more than a night here and there, but that was their arrangement. And they'd had a lot of good times together. One of his best friends on the circuit was married because the two of them set him up with Candy's best friend.

Damn, he hated that this hurt her.

"I'm so sorry for all this shit," he said. "I hope people aren't being too hard on you after that fucking video surfaced. We had the attorneys take it down, but I know the damage has already been done."

"Not your fault, hon," she said quietly. "Not at all."

"Are you okay, though?" He gripped the steering wheel, waiting for her answer. "Tell me the truth now."

"I'm fine, just a little drama, that's all. You know what this place is like. People hate you one minute and love you the next. I'm sure another scandal will be coming right around the corner. I can't be the center of attention forever."

"I hope you're right," he said. "Seriously though, is there anything you need?"

"I'm fine," she said. "You?"

"Hanging in there," he said. "The same, just waiting for it to all blow over. And hoping I don't get fired in the meantime."

"But everything's going to be okay, right?" She sounded worried. "I'm sure this kinda thing happens all the time."

"Right," he pretended to agree. "All the time."

When he ended the call, that sinking feeling returned. Tenfold. And all he could do was wait for the other shoe to drop.

As Jarod continued his drive, he thought about the other conversations he'd need to have. He knew a call to his mother was imminent, but even more disturbing was the confrontation he was sure to have with Gina. She'd have his balls for this one for sure. Not that he owed her anything. As far as he was concerned, the debt had been paid long ago. He questioned all the time if it was worth it, selling his soul, but it had seemed like the only way at the time. And it really hadn't been that bad at first. At one point, he thought it might even work between them. Of course, that was before the ultimatums began. By this point, he had met all of her demands and they were even. He'd do almost anything for his family, he had done just that, but he was at the end of his rope with Gina and her games. If the truth came out, there wasn't much more he could do to stop it. She was toxic, and he needed to get as far away from her as possible.

He'd been better since the split. Of course, he was actually trying now. Trying to be a better man. Humble. Grateful. Responsible. Dependable. He understood the opportunity he had waiting for him this time around. He could feel it. His racing had never been better. He was focused. He was ready. Getting rid of the baggage in his life surely helped.

The Chase was only a few months away, and he was a top contender. Jarod wanted this so bad he could taste it. His father never won the Sprint Cup, despite his winning career. In 2010, Tony Cage was well on his way, three races left, before the fatal crash at turn two. Jarod wouldn't let his mind go back there. If he did, the fear would paralyze him. He was there that day, racing with his dad—a day that started as a celebration and ended in a goddamn war zone. It happened so fast—warp speed. One minute cars were screaming along the track, and the next? Smoke and debris covered the speedway. Panicked voices cried out from his radio. Though Henry's voice was strong, unwavering, as he told him to stay the hell away from the turn. Cars were on fire, drivers stood on the asphalt unable to do anything else, medics moved at breakneck speed trying to save lives. Jarod asked Henry about his dad's car. Over and over again. He didn't answer. Out of the seventeen car pile-up, fifteen drivers walked away. But not Jarod's father. He was dead before they reached him.

It broke his entire family. Even today, neither his mama nor sister could watch his races live. Going to the track brought too many painful memories to the surface. But they came back from their grief closer, and no matter what kind of jams Jarod had gotten into over the past five years, his family's devotion never faltered. Still, he questioned if they could weather this latest storm.

Jarod wanted to go all the way this time, not just make it to the Chase. He was going to take the cup. He'd do it for his dad, for his mother. Hell, he'd do it for *himself* so he could finally prove he was worthy and not some fuckup who rode on Daddy's coattails.

Up until this point, he'd been good. But for a guy like Jarod, two months without sex was like a lifetime. And when he ran into an old *friend* at the bar where he was having one last hurrah before the championship season began, he couldn't say no.

He didn't *want* to say no.

That was the kind of arrogance that usually got him into these situations. Well, that, and thinking with his dick.

Speaking of…he also had Vivian to contend with.

He really thought his plan would help him shove the dark-haired beauty out of his system. It was the way he worked. Each time someone wanted something from him, he'd take something back. It was the only way to stay sane when people were always trying to take a piece of him. Too bad with Vivian his MO actually had the opposite effect. Rather than working her out of his system, he had pulled her in. All he could think about the rest of the way home was how her body curled up against his like she was designed just for him. Or the way she responded to both his offerings and his demands. Fuck, he could still smell her on his fingers. And as much as he wanted to do the smart thing this time, he knew the truth about how this would play out.

The little taste of her in the coat closet wasn't going to be enough. No, he needed to have her completely before he'd be rid of her. But he couldn't allow himself to indulge in that fantasy. At least not yet.

He had less than twenty-four hours to himself before the goddamn circus came to town. Viv had already informed the media of the press conference tomorrow, so the vultures were at bay for the time being. He was going to savor every last minute of it.

As the buildings, and crowds, and cars faded away in his rearview mirror, his mind slowed and he could breathe easier. And once he passed the old wooden Cotton Creek sign, relief warmed his belly. He was almost there.

He drove down Main Street, slowing his truck down to twenty. The quaint passage through town looked as though Uncle Sam threw up all over the place. Red, white, and blue covered every surface. His hometown was notorious for its Independence Day celebration.

Jarod waved at the Clarks as they crossed the street with their ice cream cones and toddler in tow, and honked at the children decorating their bikes for tomorrow's parade. They, in return, stuck out their tongues and made funny faces at him.

He smiled as the cloud hanging over his head began to break up and let the sun in.

Down the long gravel road, rows of tulip trees welcomed Jarod home as he pulled into his haven after the hellish ride. He got out of his truck and wanted nothing more than to grab a six-pack, go down to the dock, and cast a line. But his damn phone rang before he reached his front door. When he glanced at the screen, he immediately felt another throbbing headache coming on.

"Are you a moron?" the voice at the other end of the phone echoed in his ear when he answered.

Yep, looked like his sister was up to speed on the events of the past forty-eight hours.

Fucking perfect.

"Hello, Kate," Jarod said, taking a seat on the front porch. "And how are you this fine evening?"

"Do you know who leaked it?" she asked. Kate wasn't one for pleasantries.

Katherine Cage, a tough woman very well versed in the area of celebrity thanks to her only brother, took no prisoners when it came to protecting him. She was a financial planner and managed all of his money, which meant he was taken care of for life. Still, Jarod wasn't ready to start cashing out yet. Plus he was more interested in taking care of his family for life, and that meant he needed a few more wins under his belt.

"I have my suspicions," Jarod told her, feeling about as low as a moron—who, incidentally, was caught bare-assed for the world to see—could go. "But I don't want you to worry about that now. I got myself into this mess. I'll get out of it."

"Well, I sure hope someone on that crack team you have at the garage has a plan to help."

There was no keeping this from her. She'd just badger him until she got the answers she was looking for.

"We met with a new PR firm today," he said. "Henry says they're the best."

"You need the best right now," Kate replied. "You also

need to get that head of yours screwed on straight."

Ah, the sweet sensation of being kicked when you're down.

Jarod's sister had perfected this move.

"I know," he said as he squeezed the bridge of his nose. "I'm so sorry for embarrassing you. And—"

"I'm not finished," Kate interrupted. "You know I'd do anything to protect you. I'm always on your side. And I'm sorry you've had your share of assholes taking advantage of you lately. But you need to get your shit together, and fast."

"I know," he repeated with a scowl. She was right. Per usual. "Does Mama know yet?"

"How do you think I found out?" she said.

Jarod thought he detected a smile in her voice. Oh yeah, little sis was definitely getting a kick out of this. That meant she also thought the mess was fixable, which was a very good thing. Kate had the best instincts. Still, it didn't do much to relieve the tension in his neck knowing that his own mother watched him get nasty in a bathroom stall.

"Shit," he said, cringing. "Then why didn't she call?"

"Well, the creep factor of a mother seeing her son's sex tape online is a little high. Even for her. She thought it'd be better if I called."

"Of course, have Ms. Sensitive handle it." He stood up, opened the door, and headed toward the kitchen…and his waiting beer.

"You're a big boy now." Kate laughed. "You don't need my hand-holding. You just need a good smack up against the head."

"Man, you don't even seem fazed that my behind has been all over the internet," Jarod said, trying to make light of the situation. Because if he didn't, he'd go crazy trying to figure out who did this to him. "You have bigger cajones than I give you credit for."

"I wouldn't go that far." She verbally shuddered. "Pretty sure I'm permanently damaged from this one."

"Shit," Jarod said when his second line buzzed in his ear again. It was Henry. "Gotta take this, Katie."

"Okay, big brother," she said, this time with a trace of sadness in her words. "I'll send you my therapy bill. Love you."

"Love you, too," he said. "Be sure to tell Mama everything is fine and I'll call her in the morning."

Jarod clicked his phone over to get the latest update from Henry.

"What is it, Henry?" he said, cracking open his beer.

"Sorry to bother you after this day from hell," Henry said, his voice slow and rough.

"Don't pussyfoot around." Jarod took a long pull from the bottle. "Just tell me what it is."

"Okay, buddy, but you're not going to like it."

• • •

For the next few hours, Viv was able to work in her office without distraction. Not counting her body's constant reminders of what transpired in this very room earlier. Jarod's quid pro quo had her tight, sore, and, God help her, absolutely ravenous for more. This was so not how it was supposed to go down. Still, she mostly kept on task. She was confident the press conference would go off without incident and her new client would be well on his way to becoming the new and improved Jarod Cage, version 2.0.

Not that there was a damn thing wrong with the current package.

On the rare moments Viv did let her mind wander, she couldn't help but remember the touch of his rough hands or the way he had looked at her, drinking her in. She heard his filthy words ping around her head, and felt his breath on the shell of her ear.

The simple memory had goose bumps skating down her arms and moisture pooling between her legs.

One-time thing, Viv.

That's all it was. All it could be. But damn if he wasn't like a bag of potato chips—the delicious sea salt and vinegar kind where just one wouldn't do. That reminded her, she hadn't eaten a thing since this morning…and she was starving.

She bought a soda, a bag of chips, and two chocolate bars from the vending machine and settled in for a long night.

Not two minutes later, her phone rang.

"Join me in my office," Miranda said when she picked up.

She wished Jarod were there to see that. Viv wasn't the only one who cut right to the chase around here. Obeying her boss's command, she left her office and maneuvered around the vacant cubicles toward the lion's den.

Miranda waved her inside, but they were quickly interrupted by the Weasel. God, he was like a spoiled child desperate for Mommy's attention.

"Here are the sponsor letters you asked for, Miranda," Fredrick said.

"Sponsor letters?" Viv asked.

"Yes," Miranda said, taking the papers and quickly transferring over the copy onto her stationery. Miranda was old school and insisted on personalized correspondence. She wrote fast and fluidly, with the most beautiful penmanship. Without looking up, she continued, "I'm sending a note to the executives at Saturn to tell them how excited we are to be working with their driver. We have more than just one constituent to make happy with this case."

"Right," she said, though she never would have thought of that herself. "I could've done that, Fredrick." She didn't like how close he was to this case and felt increasingly territorial where Jarod was concerned.

"That's okay," he said, so convincingly genuine it made her sick. "I know you were *very* busy today and I didn't want to interrupt."

Shit, was he the person knocking on the door earlier?

"Well, thank you," she said. "I appreciate your help. I'm sure you did a much better job with it than I could have done." She hated having to suck up to him, but on the off chance he knew what was going on in her office today, it was well worth the shot to her pride.

He beamed and left her alone with Miranda.

"So as I was saying, we have many people that we need to keep happy with this case."

"Yes," Viv said. "Thank you for taking care of the sponsor, but I promise you I can handle the rest."

"I'm happy to hear that, because you'll need to stay close to the advertisers, the racing publications, and media, as well as the NASCAR execs."

"Absolutely. I'm on it. I've had several conference calls with many of them already."

"That's good," Miranda said. "But it's not enough. You need to meet them face-to-face. You need to be part of the Cage team. So once he heads out on the circuit, you need to be at his side."

"Oh." It was all she could think to say. She knew there would be some travel for this case, but to go out on the road? "Are you sure? I mean I can fly out to the big races. I'll need to be there for all of the events we have planned, but I think I can do a lot of this remotely."

Spending time with media and marketing people was fine, but how the hell was she supposed to be that close to Jarod? And for the next two months? This was a disaster waiting to happen.

"It's not up for negotiation, Vivian. So make all the necessary arrangements you must to make this work."

"What about my other clients?"

"You can Skype with the team here on your downtime and pass things off as you need to."

"But—" Viv began forming her arguments.

"We're done here." Miranda cut her off and went back to her computer while Viv sulked in private.

PR Rule Number 11: Know when to hold 'em and when to fold 'em.

The decision had been made, and there was nothing she could do about it.

Chapter Five

Viv worked late into the evening, not only on Jarod's case, but also to get everything in order so she could go on the road with him. For the next few months, she'd only be home a few days each week, so that meant getting organized. She paid a few bills in advance, stopped her magazine subscriptions, and sent a note to her landlord asking him to help keep an eye on the place.

By the next morning, she was back in the office to finalize the details for the press conference. Her head was still spinning. She was going to be traveling all over the country with the man who gave her the best orgasm of her life—with his fingers. She could only imagine what he could do with the rest of his body. That thought made her tingle in some very inconvenient places, especially when she was on the phone with her mom.

"This is all so exciting, Vivi," her mom said. "You must've really blown them away during the meeting."

"Not at all." She laughed, even though the memory was anything but funny. "I almost blew it. More than once. I'm afraid I might be over my head with this one. And if I don't do this right, I might blow my chance for New York. Not to mention how I could mess this up for Jarod. His career is on the line here."

"Jarod, is it?" her mother's voice sang. Viv could practically see the smirk on her face. "You sound awfully passionate about your, what did you call him earlier? Oh yes, *redneck client*."

"That was before I met him," she said. "He's not so bad. Anyway, enough about work. I was calling to see how your Fourth of July plans are coming along. Are you and Dad expecting a lot of people today?"

"A nice group," she said. "About five couples. Jenny and Rick are coming, too."

"Really?" Viv was shocked. Normally, the holiday was reserved for Dad's colleagues. Plus her father never liked her mom's friend Jenny. It was hard to believe they were going to mix company. "That's great. I hope Dad is helping you with the food and everything."

Viv hated how her father was so demanding of her mother. At least when she lived with them, she could voice her opinion when her mother wouldn't. She worried that once she left, he'd trample all over her. But lately, Corrine Blake had surprised her.

"We're going very casual this year," her mom said, no trace of anxiety that usually came with these gatherings. "Dad's grilling the burgers and brats, so all I have to do is make a few salads and dessert. Still, I wish you were here, honey."

What on earth was going on at the Blake household? Viv wanted to hear more, but the clock was ticking and she still had a million things to do.

"I do, too," she told her mom. And she did; holidays made being away from home even more difficult than normal. "But it sounds like you're going to have a great time. I'll call you before I head out on the circuit. Love you."

Viv went back to finalize everything for the press conference. They would hold it at the Atlanta Motor Speedway, trying to steer clear of the Charlotte Circus, as Jarod called it. This way, it would be a more controlled, smaller crowd. And it was a perfect lead-in to the charity event she had planned for later. She had to pull quite a few strings and enlist Henry's help, but she was able to arrange a special day for the Kids of Valor, an organization that helped children of fallen or injured soldiers. They had over a dozen children ready to come out to spend time with Jarod and do a few ride-alongs.

What she hadn't known was that he did this kind of thing all the time, especially for his local chapter in South Carolina. Why someone hadn't been playing up his role with the kids was beyond her.

Viv felt Miranda's eyes burn a hole through the top of her head before the Ice Queen even entered the room. She really needed to put some kind of GPS system on that woman. Miranda was always catching her off guard.

She jumped up from her ergonomically designed chair, a necessity with the kind of hours she kept, and with her smile secure, she greeted her boss. "Miranda, come in. How are you this morning?"

Miranda didn't answer what Viv felt was a gracious

salutation. No surprise there. Instead, she dangled a chain of keys from her claws.

Now what?

Miranda sauntered in and dropped the keys on the desk—a noise that made the permanent metal retainer behind Viv's lower teeth zing.

She met her boss's frosty gaze.

"I'm sure you caught the *Race Way* this morning?" she said.

Shit, shit, double shit.

"Sorry, no. I've been preparing for the client press conference."

Miranda closed her eyes and took a breath, mimicking an exasperated mother dealing with a disobedient child. Viv knew exactly how she felt; she also knew a chastising of epic proportions was unavoidable.

"What happened?" she asked with a wince.

"You'd know if you did the simple things asked of you at the kickoff. You must read the *Race Way* every day—throughout the day. It is the *New York Times* of NASCAR. Bookmark it on all of your devices. Keep it open on your browser. Jesus, Vivian, this is basic PR101. Please don't tell me I made a mistake putting you on lead."

"No. No, ma'am, you didn't," she said, trying for her best Southern charm. It came off as a sarcastic teen. "It was an oversight. Won't happen again."

"Go, read up on the latest crisis," Miranda barked. "Then go pack a bag and get to Mr. Cage's home immediately after the event."

"Wait. What?"

Either Viv's caffeine hadn't kicked in yet, or Miranda

just told her she was having a sleepover with Jarod tonight.

"I thought we went over this last night," Miranda said, scrolling through emails on her phone, clearly bored with this conversation.

Looks like it was the latter.

"No, we talked about the races only," she argued, slowing her speech in an effort to settle her temper.

"I've talked to Mr. Cage's manager and his sponsors, and we all agree, there is more work that needs to be done before he gets back on the racetrack. He can't keep coming to Atlanta for council, so you'll need to work at his home and then accompany him to the race."

"Miranda," she said, clicking her pen over and over again, like she was a junkie with a morphine pump. Sadly, her pen didn't dispense any drugs to calm her. "I can't do that. I mean, stay at a client's house? This whole thing seems a little much for a working relationship."

"Maybe," Miranda said, switching her attention from her nails to her phone. "If there weren't"—she looked up now—"*millions* of dollars on the line."

Viv's hands began to sweat. This was only the second time she ever questioned her boss, and she was finding out it wasn't for the faint of heart.

"Yes, but—"

Miranda stopped her there. "You want to work in this business? You do what needs to be done. No ifs, ands, or buts. This is what the job entails, and if you can't do it, good Lord, tell me now. We've already wasted enough time."

"No," Viv said. "I can do this."

"Are you sure?" Miranda mocked her. "I know this wasn't in your job description."

"I'm sure," she said, but it came out in a whisper.

Miranda acted like this was business as usual, and it was perfectly normal for her to stay with Jarod at his home and then follow him around the track during race weekends.

Too shocked for words, Viv sat there numb and silent as Miranda went on about strategy, messaging, and media training. None of it sank in. She couldn't get past the part where she had somehow become part of the Cage entourage.

"Oh," Miranda added. "You should know, Mr. Cage is not at all pleased with this situation, so it's up to you to make him comfortable."

Well, that was just peachy.

Once Miranda left her office, Viv slammed down another pot of coffee, talked herself out of a nervous breakdown, and tried to put the upcoming sleepover out of her mind. It was the only way she was going to get through the day.

She mindfully set her list of priorities. At the top? Addressing the latest media crisis. Viv pulled up the online trade publication and went to work. The cover story was a video package about Bathroom Sex Girl, Candace Ford. She was caught by a celebrity gossip show—one of those crude programs designed to provoke celebrities into saying something stupid. The reporter pretty much harassed the woman, calling her a home-wrecker. Then they cut to a shot of Gina McKnight—a raven-haired beauty who seemed just a tad too sexy to work for ESPN. Or maybe that was the point.

"I can't talk about this right now," she said, batting her teary eyes to the camera, apparently still playing the jilted fiancée.

It might have fooled the racing world, but Viv knew an act when she saw one. Hell, she invented the teary-eyed glance to the camera. "Please just give us our privacy as we handle this personal matter."

There was Gina taking the high road. It was so civilized. So emotional. So very contrived.

Still, it just made Jarod look worse, and she couldn't have that, so she immediately began rewriting his speech in her head. They would nip this in the bud ASAP.

Chapter Six

Jarod arrived at the track early and in much better spirits than the day before. Despite their rough start, he was starting to believe that Viv was the right person for the job. He trusted her for some reason, and that wasn't something to be taken lightly in his world.

The guys in the garage had the cars ready to go for the kids' event, and Jarod thought he'd take them for a spin before the media showed up. Henry convinced him that they could easily combine the press conference with an event for the Kids of Valor, so Jarod agreed. Something good may as well come out of this day. He loved the kids, and the guys did an excellent job with the ride-along cars. The little buggers would get a kick out of it.

Jarod grew up on the track and could still remember his first trip to the speedway, his first ride, the first race that took his breath away. Even as a child, he couldn't get enough of the smell of oil and burned rubber in the air, the roaring of the engines, the feel of dirt on his hands, and the naughty words he heard hanging out with the crew in the garage. It was heaven for a rambunctious little boy. But it was more than that. It was his safe place, where he could be near his dad. It was one experience he loved to share.

And after he was finished making memories with the kids, he had a special surprise waiting for Vivian. She needed an initiation into NASCAR pronto, and he knew just how to do it.

"What are you doing?" Vivian came barreling into his sacred place and shot his plan to shit.

Gone was that blissed-out woman from yesterday. In her place? The sour pixie with a stick up her ass.

"I've been looking for you forever," she snapped. "We need to rehearse in the press room and get you looking presentable."

Presentable?

"I look just fine, and we have plenty of time to rehearse," he said, trying to kill the negative energy around her.

It didn't help. They walked up to the pressroom, and Vivian continued ordering him around, being a genuine pain in the ass. She had clothes picked out for him to wear, not to mention a hairstylist and makeup artist. Hell if he was going to put that shit on his face. She had the words for him to say and even picked out the place they would stand.

"I'll introduce you," she said. "You'll join us through this door. Nod a few times to the members of the press and stand right here."

She wanted to plan his gestures, too? What in the actual fuck?

"Also, be sure to look straight ahead. Don't look up as

you're trying to form your words—it makes you look guilty. And don't fidget."

"Hold up there, Yank." Jarod gritted his teeth, trying to keep his temper in check. "I've done dozens of press conferences before."

"Not like this one, you haven't."

"Maybe not, but I can handle my own clothes and hair, and the way I stand." He tried to play it cool, but the anger grew. Who the hell did she think she was? "And if you think I'm going to put any girlie shit on my face, you are out of your fucking mind."

"This is my show," she said in that goddamn combative tone she liked to use. "And we are going to do this my way."

The balls on this woman. It was almost comical how she tried to lay down the law. But enough was enough. It was time to cut her off at the pass and make her slow that fine ass down.

Jarod took a calming breath. This was a woman who couldn't be barked at, or intimidated, or told what's what. She needed to be handled—delicately yet firmly—like his prized Ferrari.

"Hey now, hold up a minute." He flashed the grin he reserved for occasions such as this. "I'd like a restart. Can we do that?"

"I'm sorry, Jarod, but we don't have time for chitchat. Save it for your boys in the garage. I'm sure they'd love to shoot the breeze with you."

"Well, yes, that's true. I am quite a conversationalist, but at the moment, I'd like to speak with you."

"Can you do me a favor and wait until *after* I save your career?"

So fiery, this one. Yet he knew it was an act. She was clearly freaking out, and God help him, he wanted to make it better. Too bad he only had one tool in his toolbox.

"What's got that lacy thong in a bunch this morning?" He moved in closer, so his arm brushed against hers. Damn, that was going to cost him. "It is lace again, isn't it?"

"Please don't," she whispered, but her eyes dilated, betraying her.

That's better.

He took another step closer.

"Don't you start," she threatened, holding out a hand to prevent him from advancing any closer.

She was on the edge, and it was all he could do not to take her against the wall in the pressroom. They both needed it. Still, now was not the time.

"What is it?" he asked, changing direction. "Talk to me. I'm sure it can't be any worse than what I have to do later. With my mother and nana looking on, I might add."

"Yes, you're right." Her eyes warmed. "I should be consoling you. It's just I've been up all night preparing for this, and then I see your fake fiancée on the *Race Way* this morning, playing the wronged woman. I'll tell you, I already detest her skinny ass. We have to go after her."

"Can't," he said, though he wanted to give her more.

"What does that mean?" she asked. "I can't do my job if you don't let me in. So just tell me, are you going to be straight with me or not?"

"I've been nothing but straight with you. Look, I said things were complicated with Gina. I can't control what she says or does, and I'm not going to address it."

"You have to address it."

"No, I don't. I'm sorry, but that's just the way it has to be for now."

"Look," she said, pushing the script into his hands. "I made a change to your statement. Not a big deal. It's still short and to the point."

Jarod read it and shook his head. "Not saying this part about my relationship. Trust me on this. For most drivers, privacy is allowed. Encouraged even. Most of this personal stuff stays out of the press, so it's not going to look weird or suspicious if I don't acknowledge it. I will say I'm sorry for my behavior. I will promise to do better. But the rest is off the table."

"Why can't you just do as I ask?" she huffed.

"Well, for one, you don't ask nicely. You are such a Yank in that way. You steamroll in and take no finesse with what you say or how you say it. It's just so damn abrasive. And rude."

"You're calling me rude?"

"Yep," he said, distracting her from the Gina situation. "Afraid I am. Also, I'm not pimping out the kids' charity event for this shit show."

"Oh, yes you are. I planned this."

"Henry said—"

Viv shrugged.

"You're in cahoots with my manager now?" He crumpled the new script in his hand. "That's how we're going to play it?"

"I'm not playing anything." She reached in her folder and pulled out a new copy of the speech, waving it in his face. Of course she had extras. "I'm working to get your ass out of this sling and back on the track."

He knew she was right. He might not like it, but he did believe she knew how to play the game.

"Your job isn't the only one on the line here," she said unexpectedly. "I have a lot riding on this, too, so please follow my lead."

"What do you mean, 'your job isn't the only one on the line'?" He didn't like the sound of that at all.

"I'm not going to discuss it." She pushed the new script at him again.

"You are," he snapped. Then he crossed his arms, leaned against the wall, and waited, until she finally caved.

"I'm up for a transfer to New York," she said. "Miranda's been holding me back, but she's told me that if I get you to the Chase, I will get my transfer."

"And that's important to you?" he asked.

"It's all I've wanted since I graduated from college."

Jarod took the script and considered her. "All right, Viv. But you know how it goes. If I do this for you…"

"For us. Don't forget, *you* are going to get the most benefit out of the deal."

"Okay, woman. If I do this *for us*, there's something you can do for us as soon as the kids' event is over."

"No way." She took two steps backward and put up her palms. "I will not be doing *that* with you ever again."

"Don't flatter yourself, doll. I have something else in mind."

"Fine," Vivian said. "Let's just get through the day, and I'll do whatever it is you need me to do so we stay even-steven. Man, your parents must've had a heck of a time with you. Each time, your sister got a lollipop, you had to get a lollipop. I bet your dad—" She stopped dead in her tracks.

Jarod was wondering how long it would take before the

General came into conversation. "My dad what?" he asked.

"Dammit, I'm sorry," Viv said. "I didn't mean to bring him up. You're right, sometimes I get going and I don't think. I've read about your dad, and I can't imagine how hard it was for all of you to lose him that way. I know you think I'm an insensitive and tactless Yankee, but I do have a heart."

"Hey now," Jarod said in a soft voice, feeling guilty for cutting into her. "I don't think that of you. And you can talk about my dad. I'm okay hearing about him. It's even nicer talking about him outside of racing. Truth is, he didn't make things even between Kate and me. Dad was pretty old school and saw it as our job—the men's job—to make sure the ladies of the house were happy. He started toughening me up by the time I was five or so. He was hardly home, so he wanted to be sure I would be around to help my mom."

"That must have been hard," Viv said. "You were so little."

"It was what it was." He shrugged. "Still, I had a great childhood. My mom is the best, and the time we did get with Dad was special. And when he wasn't around, I had the guys. Henry always made time for me." Jarod took her notebook and pen and set them down on the table. They needed to go out and get some fresh air.

"Enough of all the heavy shit," he said. For a moment, he considered wrestling her phone out of her hand as well, but knew she'd never give that up. "We have a big day ahead, and we have plenty of time before the press arrives. Let me show you around the place."

Viv's eyes tracked the room, and he could tell how hard it was for her to let go. "Are you sure? I think I'd feel better if we went through your speech a few times."

"I think we'd feel better with a walk. Forget about all

of this for a few minutes. You really need to listen to me on that. All this stuff will eat you up if you let it. You need to learn when to let it be and walk away."

"Okay," Viv said.

"Okay."

Jarod hadn't expected to launch into a big sob story, but Viv made it easy. He even found that talking to her was actually enjoyable. Despite her down-to-business demeanor, she was kind. And he didn't come across that very often in his line of work.

They started the tour in the stands and worked their way infield. Jarod told Viv about the history of the speedway and the drivers who raced there. He even rattled off a few of his wins at this particular track. It was a little pathetic, but he wanted to impress her.

Viv looked around the complex in wonder. She looked at *him* in wonder, now that he thought about it. He liked that. Very much.

"I take it you've never been to a track," he said. "Or a race, for that matter."

"Sorry," she said. "Forgive me?"

"It's okay." He knew he was pushing his luck, but he was unable to prevent the next words that fell out of his mouth. "I'm happy to be the one to pop your cherry."

Jarod was captivated watching Viv as three things happened simultaneously. She shuddered and shifted her feet, and her nipples pebbled under her shirt.

It was the exact reaction he was looking for. He wasn't sure why, but making her squirm was so fucking enjoyable. And after their deep moments, it was time to lighten things up.

"What did we say about the bad-boy routine?" Viv asked when she found her breath.

"Hey, I never agreed to anything." Jarod swore she shifted her feet again. "I am what I am."

"You got that right." Viv smacked his chest. "Now reel it in, Cage, and take me to the pit road."

"There is so much I have to teach you." Jarod ran a tough, calloused hand down her arm. "The first thing I'm going to teach you is the basic NASCAR lexicon. It's not called *the* pit road. It's simply pit road."

"Now who's the uptight one?"

"I'm just protecting you, baby. I don't want you to say the wrong thing and look like a fool."

"Aw, how kind of you." Viv rolled her eyes, but he could see the tension was already lifting.

For the next thirty minutes, Jarod took her on a tour. They walked in the grandstands and he pointed out the obnoxious condos, showed her the special car he'd drive the kids around in, and introduced her to his people. He knew this was technically business, but it felt more like pleasure. Hell, he felt like a goddamn kid in a candy store. He was giddy, and he needed to get a serious grip.

Even stranger? It looked as if Viv was actually enjoying herself.

"I can't believe you've been in Atlanta for over two years and have never been to AMS," he said. "You know they call it a modern motorsports palace."

"I can see why." She winked. "Seriously though, I don't really get why drivers like this place so much. What makes one track so different from the others? What's so great about it?"

"So, so many things," Jarod said, honestly trying to tone it down. "One indicator is the number of close finishes in a race. That's what racing is all about, right? The excitement of the cars neck-and-neck to the very end. Some of the best chases and best finishes have been at AMS. The track's rough and has character. The multiple grooves help grip the tires and make it a blast to drive on. You can fly on this track."

You'll see.

They made their way infield and Jarod bored her in the garage. She was a good sport, not a smart-ass remark to be had. He liked having her there with him, and realized he had never taken a woman to one of his races. Gina had been around when she was working or desperate to make a scene, but other than that, there'd been nobody else. He was thinking it might be something he wanted to change.

Until he caught the pit crew ogling her.

That disturbed him more than he cared to admit.

After the tour, Viv kicked it into high gear. She left him to greet the reporters, setting up his grand entrance and providing the press with his upcoming schedule of charity events. He was set to arrive at exactly 2:05. So he stayed in the garage and paced until it got close, reading her text messages that provided the play-by-play of who was there and the questions they were asking.

She said they'd keep it short and agreed that after he made the statement, he didn't have to take any questions. That's why she planned the event directly after. Though it may not have been the best timing, hanging out with kids just days after the leaked sex tape made the news, it was the type of event Jarod did all the time. So he felt good getting back to business as usual.

"Good afternoon," Jarod began after entering the pressroom at precisely 2:05. "Thank you all for coming and listening to what I have to say today. As many of you know, a video of a very personal nature was posted online without my consent this week. And while I'm very concerned with this invasion into my life, I'm also concerned and aware of the impact this situation has had on my business, my partners, my owners—Chip Scott Racing, my crew, and my sponsors, especially the Saturn Corp. But most importantly, the effect it's had on my family, friends, fans, and the sport of NASCAR. Though this was a private matter, I shouldn't have been so careless and I take full responsibility for my actions. This is not what I want to be known for. This is not how I want to live my life. It was a lapse in judgment, and I can tell you, it will never happen again."

That was it, all he was supposed to say, but for the first time in his life, Jarod thought he owed them more. Vivian stood up, fidgeting and subtly gesturing for him to leave the podium, but he continued to talk.

"This was my wake up call, y'all, and let me tell you, the message has been received. I have a bright future in this sport, and I have so much to give back. My team and sponsors are the best, and we have a car that can take it all this year. I am not going to jeopardize that. And I will give NASCAR fans a heck of a show in the weeks ahead. Thank you."

Judging by Vivian's expression, he did just fine. She gave him a nod and stepped up to the stage right as the media began firing questions.

"What about Gina?" one reporter called out.

That's when Jarod left and Vivian jumped in. He'd never been so grateful in his life.

"We're not here to talk about anyone other than Mr. Cage," she said.

"What would the General say?" another asked.

"I'm not going to answer such an insensitive question. So if you have nothing else to ask about Mr. Cage, we'll conclude this press conference."

Just like that, the tone changed and the reporters asked about the upcoming races. Vivian handled it like a pro.

She said it went as well as could be expected. The holiday made for a short news cycle, and the Jarod Cage sex tape would be old news by the following race.

So now they had a bit of breathing room. The most difficult part was over, she said. Jarod desperately wanted to believe it.

• • •

While Vivian finished up with the press, Jarod went down to the garage, changed into his gear, and talked with the crew. They had a nice pace car ready for the kids. And something a little more exciting for Viv's turn. She thought racing was a never-ending series of left turns? Well, she was partially right about that. But he was happy to be the one to enlighten her to the rest of it.

Vivian met him in the garage, kids marching in a line right behind her. She looked a bit like a schoolteacher. A smoking hot, unavailable, unattainable teacher. And there went his mind, straight into the damn gutter.

Easy, Cage. Easy.

He'd been too distracted with the press conference earlier to fully appreciate her outfit. A pale yellow skirt and silk blouse. What did she call that look? Business fuckable?

Whatever the hell it was, he approved.

"Kids," Vivian announced when they made their way inside. "This is Mr. Cage. He drives the number nine Toyota on the NASCAR circuit and he's ready to make you all race car drivers for the day."

Wow, she even introduced him the proper way. The kids cheered, and Jarod felt an unidentifiable pull in his chest. He found that focusing on her ass, instead of the whole package, was the only way he'd be able to keep that sensation unidentifiable. So that's what he did.

He showed the kids around, let them play with the tools, holding out any mention of the ride until the very end. Any time any of the kids would ask, he'd say, "A ride? I have no idea what you're talking about."

His teasing also gave Vivian a few more reasons to smack him, push him, or jab at his chest. Anything to get her to put her hands on him.

"Okay," he finally gave in, secretly deciding he'd give the quiet boy in glasses the first ride. The boy knew all the stats of the drivers and the points in the season, as well as a ridiculous amount of information about his cars. It was impressive, but it was all cerebral for him. It reminded him of someone else he knew.

Jarod couldn't wait to take both of them for a spin.

"Harrison, you are my lucky copilot today," he said.

Harrison's eyes grew wide, but he didn't say a word.

"You okay with that, dude?" Jarod asked.

The boy nodded.

"Okay, then." Jarod worried the poor kid might hurl in his car. "Go with Jimmy over there, and he'll get you geared up."

The boy walked on wobbly legs. Jarod might have to take this one a little slower than the others.

"What about ladies first?" the only girl in the group piped up.

Jarod instantly thought of her as a young Vivian.

"Ladies ride on the roof in NASCAR," he deadpanned.

"Watch it, Cage," Jarod's friend Joanne said as she walked in from the adjoining garage.

The little girl squealed once Joanne Black joined the group. Joanne was the best female driver in NASCAR. A helluva driver by either gender's standard, though not all the guys had the balls to admit it. Jarod called in a favor once he noticed there was a girl in the group. He thought she'd get a kick out of riding with Jo.

And maybe he thought it might score him a few points with Vivian as well.

"Go on with Joanne," Jarod said to the girl. "And then you come back to ride with me and I'll show you how it's really done." He flashed a wink, and the girl stuck her tongue out at him.

Jarod drove Harrison around the track five times without any fluids leaving his body. The boy was scared shitless, but he wasn't going to let anyone else know it. In fact, the little guy joined in the trash talk with the other boys as they waited their turns.

That's the way, kid.

He took his time with each child, making sure they got their money's worth. But he was the one who always got the most out of it. He loved their excitement—how they were so open to new things and wanted nothing more than to have fun. No ulterior motives, no hidden agendas. Plus, they hadn't had the chance to become jaded yet. They gave him…hope.

He went thirty minutes over the allotted time for the event. That was nothing new. He expected Vivian to be bored to tears or punching away on that phone of hers. Turned out, he'd misjudged her again. She was laughing with the kids, the phone nowhere to be found.

"Well, that was awesome," Viv said when the last rug rat made his way off the infield. "You're really good with kids."

"Thanks," he said, somewhat embarrassed. A rare emotion for him. Sex tape notwithstanding. "It was a good day all the way around."

"It was," she agreed.

"It's not over yet," Jarod reminded her.

"That's right," she said. "My surprise."

"Your surprise."

"Are you taking me for a ride?"

Jarod wiggled his eyebrows. He honestly couldn't help messing with her. Though it might have seemed like he was being playful, there was nothing innocent about his intentions.

"In the pace car," she clarified.

"I *am* taking you for a ride," he said, clearing his throat and shifting to racing mode. He couldn't let his dick get in the way of her safety.

"But first we need to get you geared up." He walked her to the restroom in the garage and handed her a fire suit and the base layer that goes underneath. "Here you go, change into this. Keep your skivvies on, then put on the base layer, and then the suit."

Yes, he would do something about all the sexual tension between them. Later.

"Yay, we get to be twinsies." Vivian clapped.

"Say that again, and you will never ride in my car."

"Isn't Jimmy going to get me geared up?" she asked, pushing him.

"Not today." Jarod placed his hands on her shoulders, spinning her toward the bathroom door. He fucking loved that she shivered at his touch. That'd teach her to play with him. "Today, you're all mine. Now go get dressed."

"Seriously?" Viv asked. "It's hot as Hades out here. Do I really need to change into all of this?"

"You do. I would never jeopardize that sweet little body of yours. And nobody gets into the cars without flame-retardant gear."

"You plan on setting us on fire?" She inspected the gear.

"Baby, you have no idea what can happen on pit road."

"Is that from a movie or something?" she snarked.

"I'm hurt that you have no faith in my originality. Now scoot."

Viv complained nonstop from the bathroom, while Jarod just shook his head. Once she came out, however, he was completely unprepared.

Why was it so damn sexy when a woman wore a man's things?

A jersey, a number, a baseball hat, a T-shirt for bed. The fire suit was no exception. He couldn't take his eyes off her, and something uncomfortably possessive rolled in his gut as he appraised the way the suit hugged her curves.

"How do I look?" she asked, taking a quick twirl.

"Very nice." He gritted his teeth, using every ounce of

willpower he could muster to prevent him from sporting wood in his own suit. "Are you ready for the ride of your life?"

"Ready as I'll ever be."

"Okay then, doll." He walked past her, knowing he wouldn't be able to control himself walking behind that scrumptious ass. "Follow me down to pit road."

"Stop with all the sweet talk already." Not one to be left behind, she caught up to him so they were walking side by side.

"You should know by now, I don't have a sweet bone in my body. You've seen me in action, after all."

"You're not going to get to me, Cage, so let's do this thing. Take me for a spin."

For a spin. Right.

It was time to teach her smart mouth a little lesson.

Jarod took Viv's hand and led her toward an electric-blue car. "Where's the pace car?" she asked, trying out another NASCAR term.

"Has someone been studying?" he asked. "A little NASCAR 101?"

"I'm a very good student," she said. "But there's only so much you can learn by the book. Come on, show me the ropes."

"Okay, but we're not going in the pace car." He pulled her along.

"Why not?"

"It's for babies. I'm giving you're the real experience, the closest thing you can get to driving in a real race."

"Is it safe?"

"You should know that we don't often use words like that around here. Nothing's safe, baby. Nothing."

Chapter Seven

Jarod wore a blue fire suit that highlighted his cerulean eyes, which were now blazing with heat. And when he brushed his unkempt hair out of them, they flashed in her direction, making her panties instantly grow damp.

She appreciated the distraction because, if truth be told, she was nervous to get into Jarod's death trap, especially when she found out they weren't taking the same car he used with the kids. This was definitely a more souped-up version.

If that was even a thing.

Viv's skin sizzled as he took her hand and led her toward the car. She was surprised how much she craved his touch. When it was just the two of them, everything faded into the background.

He was so confident. So in control. It was a welcome change from her typical clients. It was also hot as hell. For the entire day, she'd kept all her lustful thoughts in check. Despite all of his innuendos and raunchy ways, she'd built up a Jarod-proof dam and she was determined—damn it—not to let him burst through it. Right now, though, when he was in this element, it was impossible to keep him at bay.

"Okay, Vivian," he said in his delicious drawl, before swiping at a bead of sweat near his temple.

Leave it, she said in her head, fighting the urge to lap it up.

Viv bit the inside of her cheek to stifle her needy whimper. But when his hand gave hers a tight squeeze, her sex clenched in response. She swore to God he knew.

"Come on," he said with a wink. "It's time to kick this tour up a notch."

Viv said a quick Hail Mary as the crew guys loaded her in the death trap feetfirst. A man named Roger moved in to help her with the seat belt, but Jarod shut him down to take care of it himself.

The fumes of fuel and exhaust filled her head, and her stomach turned. For all her big talk, she was afraid of things like speed, spinning, closed-in spaces…über-sexy, controlling alpha men.

Jarod leaned over in his seat in what should've been an impossible task considering the tiny space he had to work with, to lock her in. That's how she looked at it. She was locked in. Trapped.

He was silent as he checked over her gear. She saw none of the laid-back bad boy she'd grown used to. He'd become Mr. Safety. All rules and focus. Very familiar to the way he was in her closet. Stern, determined, controlling.

Though Viv could give him a run for his money off the track—something she enjoyed a lot—she found it surprisingly easy, comfortable (even freeing—dare she admit it) to let him take control in that driver's seat. If she was being honest, she preferred it.

"I've got it, guys," Jarod said, shooing away the rest of the crew.

He checked her helmet, with his laser focus on her. He didn't meet her eyes. No, they were fixated on each task. It made her feel treasured. Important.

In addition to the helmet, her seat had a protective headrest to hold her in place. It was a little too confining for her liking, but there was no way she was going to tell Jarod that.

The seat belt came over both shoulders, and Jarod ran two gloved fingers under the strap as he brought it down over her chest, meticulously aligning it just right, leaving her every nerve ending pulsing on contract. Her breathing hitched, and she wondered why he wasn't feeling the same influx of chemicals filling the air. How could she be alone in this?

Jarod's finger grazed her breast. True, they may have been covered in a fire-retardant armor, but she could still feel him. This time, her reaction was audible.

His jaw twitched, but other than that he seemed unaffected.

He rode the seat belt over her stomach to the clasp between her legs. His knuckles lodged in the perfect place to apply the pressure she ached for.

"Not yet," he growled as though he could read her mind. In her current state, it wouldn't have been too hard to guess what she was thinking.

Jarod pulled on the straps, nodding at the taut tug of resistance. The crew put up what looked like nets on the windows, and after a few words to Henry, he started the engine.

The car trembled its way to life, and Viv could feel the sheer power of the machine.

Okay, so maybe she did get why the guys loved talking horsepower and gauges and engine-y stuff. It was pretty darn impressive.

She leaned back against the seat, which was a relief. Her head was heavy as hell in the helmet. She took a deep breath, searching for calm. The anticipation had her stomach tightening and her mouth watering. Not in a good way, either.

Please don't get sick in the car. Please.

Jarod did some signal to Henry and then tipped his head in her direction.

"You okay in there?" he asked. His mouth was covered by the helmet, so the only thing she could use to gauge expression were his deep blue eyes. They were practically twinkling.

She nodded, since she'd lost her capacity for speech once the belt clicked in place.

"On your mark," Jarod teased, turning his head to the track.

Viv froze, holding her breath, but it quickly dispelled the very next moment because he didn't finish the countdown. There was no *get set.* There was no *go.*

He hit the gas and they shot out of pit road like a rocket.

Viv had absolutely no time to prepare.

The speed of the car seemed to defy all logic. That machine jumped from zero to one hundred before Viv even realized it. She couldn't focus yet. Everything was a blur, and time was measured in breaths rather than minutes and seconds.

Her head rattled in the headrest, and she worked to hold

still so she could witness Jarod in his domain.

Breathe.

He switched gears.

Breathe.

Acceleration.

Breathe.

He worked the steering wheel as they approached the first turn. The scene in the windshield was taking shape. It was almost worse when she could see. In that moment, all she could focus on was the view directly ahead: a tiny strip of track, followed by a hill, grass, and the stadium seats. She felt like they were going to head straight off the track before he took the left. He spun the wheel, and the car did as he demanded. There was never a question. Jarod had the strongest, most capable hands of anyone she'd ever seen and she would never look at them the same way again.

Breathe.

The car rounded the turn, fast and efficient, holding on as if being pulled by a magnetic force.

Breathe.

They were back on the straightaway.

She couldn't count the number of laps. So much of the ride had been a blur. But by the last go-round, she could see everything clearly. It was the most ultimate rush. Better than sex. Well, better than Viv's experience with sex. Though she doubted she'd feel the same way if she ever made it into bed with Jarod. The coat closet episode had been enough to throw her off her axis.

The car finally began to slow, and Viv was stunned to silence.

Jarod was a force—controlled and masterful. She felt

like an idiot for making fun of his profession. She'd underestimated it. Underestimated him.

She vowed right then to never do that again.

• • •

They pulled into the garage, and once Jarod stopped the car, he took off his helmet and belt and leaned across the seat to help with hers. "You okay there?"

"Never better," she said, her voice shaking.

The guys helped Jarod out of the car and then moved to her side of the vehicle. Even in her haze, she heard him argue with the crew.

"Leave her," he told them. "I'll get her."

He reached inside, slid his hands under her arms, and pulled her from the car. She couldn't feel her legs when her feet touched the ground, and the rest of her was a trembling mess.

"It's the g-forces." He kept his arm around her as brought her inside the garage. One of the guys in the crew handed him a bottle of Gatorade. "On a few turns, we probably hit two or three g's. It's enough to mess you up. Here, try some of this."

He held the sports drink to her lips, and she gulped it down, savoring the tanginess on her tongue. "The electrolytes will set you right."

"How long were we gone?" she asked.

"About seven minutes."

"And how long are most of your races?" she asked, finishing off the drink.

"Two to three hours, depending," he said.

"And what's the temperature in that car?" Viv pulled at the fire suit, and Jarod helped her take down the top portion of it. He peeled the thick fabric from her body, unwrapping her like a birthday present. One he couldn't wait to get his hands on. Viv let out a low and raspy noise she didn't recognize as her own.

Under the top of the suit, she revealed the protective long-sleeve shirt that was similar to Under Armour. It was surprisingly cool, and she could finally breathe again.

"What's with all the questions?" he asked, doing the same with his suit.

"I'm trying to work all this out. Tell me about the temperature."

"It can get up to one hundred twenty degrees, give or take."

"That's insane."

"No." He laughed. "That's racing."

Viv felt foolish. There was so much more to the—dare she say *sport*—than she thought. And there was so much more to Jarod. She never expected him to be so respectful, thoughtful, confident…

The speed was exhilarating, unlike anything she'd ever felt. Thankfully, the drink helped replenish everything she lost in the ride, and soon she could feel the rest of her body again.

Jarod seemed to sense that exact moment when she snapped out of her stupor. He took her by the arm and pulled her into the corner of the garage. Viv followed blindly. The crew scattered around, in and out of the space, working on things and messing with the cars. Jarod settled her alongside a tall toolbox, mostly out of view. His eyes narrowed, pinning her under the weight of his gaze.

"I don't know if I trust you when you look at me like that," she said.

"Girl, you just *took a spin* in my car at speeds over one hundred fifty miles per hour. And you let me finger you in your office, for Christ's sake. I'd say *trust* is the least of our worries."

"Oh?" she asked. "Then what is the most of our worries?"

"The *most*, is trying to convince the public that our relationship is strictly business, when all I can think about is this sweet body." He resumed his attention on her fire suit, loosening the belt around her waist. What he was planning to do, she wasn't sure, but she desperately wanted to find out.

"Why?" she asked on an exhale. He could have anyone he wanted, so why would he be hung up on her?

"See, it's my curiosity that's killing me," he explained. "I haven't even had the chance to get a proper look at you. Our time in the closet—that was a tease. I mean, I know my voice can make your nipples tighter than the lug nuts on those tires over there, but what I don't know is: *What color are they?* Pale pink? Tawny? Bronze? A pretty rose, maybe? And that leads me to…"

"Don't say it." She pressed a finger to his lips.

Jarod inched closer, backing her farther into the corner. Shielding her with his body. And before she could understand what was happening, he reached his hand inside the bottom part of her suit—under both her protective leggings and her panties. Quickly, surely, he found the apex of her thighs, and the world around her ceased to exist. All she could feel was his touch through her slick arousal. All she could see was the way he flexed his jaw and worked his hand. Rough fingers opened her, while he pretended to help her after the turbulent ride around the track. She gasped and slumped against him.

"G-forces," he said loudly. "Happens to all of us."

The guys' laughter filled the garage. But to Viv, the sound was muffled, like she was underwater.

"Baby," he whispered in her ear. "You're so hot and wet right now I don't think you'd care if I stripped you out of this suit, bent you over, and bared your tight ass to the crew before I fucked you from behind."

"Pig," she said, unconvincingly. His words had successfully turned her body against her.

"I could be *your* pig for a night," he whispered before moving his other hand upward, ghosting his thumb over the nipple that pebbled under her shirt.

He was right. She didn't care who saw her. Didn't care what he did to her in front of all these men. It was madness. Complete, utter madness.

"Let me get you out of here," he said, walking her to the restroom and grabbing her bag of clothes. "Truth is, I don't want to give anyone a show. I'm selfish that way."

She wasn't sure what happened to careful, reliable Viv, but part of her liked this upgrade. A hell of a lot. Even so…

"I'm not so sure that's a good idea," she said.

"Sometimes it's best to let your body make up your mind," he said. "Don't think, just do."

"Easier said than done," Viv said once her head began to clear. "We've seen the trouble with this philosophy of yours." She tried to maintain some sort of authority, despite the fact that she now stood in the middle of the garage bathroom half naked.

"I'd never gamble with you, Vi." His voice was soft, and the way he looked at her was almost reverent.

"Vi?" she questioned, warmth pooling in her belly.

"Yeah, I think we've passed the point of formalities. I've earned the opportunity to give you my own nickname. It didn't work anyway, you know, trying to keep your distance from me. It might have made me want you more."

"We don't even know if we're compatible," she said, trying not to let his words sink in. Trying not to *feel*. "We don't know that sleeping together would solve anything."

"I think we both know that's not true," he said, toying with her hair. "But this isn't about me. It's about you. About taking what you want. So tell me, what do you want?"

She finally dared to answer. "You," she said, more throaty and porn-star-ish than she intended. And there was the truth. It was stupid, and insane, and inappropriate. But she wanted him more than she'd ever wanted any man. Her body ached for him. "Just one time."

The words were barely out of her mouth when Jared shed the rest of her clothes and let them drop to the floor. Once again, she stood before him in only her bra and panties.

Jarod used a single finger to trace an invisible line from her neck, over her décolletage and cleavage, stopping at her navel.

"Agreed." He kissed her lips lightly before attacking her breast.

The man had many different speeds—multiple gears. And he used them all strategically. Mind-numbingly fast. Achingly slow. Her body was like a car on the track, and he was in complete control.

He pulled the cup down from her right breast and gave

it a quick tug before soothing the tight bud with his warm tongue. The line between pleasure and pain blurred, and she so wanted to give in to it.

He lavished her left breast in the same way. "Just this one time," he repeated. And it somehow made her relax. They had a deal. A plan. That was smart, predictable. Thoughtful. She could live with that. And soon she was arching her back and offering him more.

"Just this one time," she repeated. "And then we'll stop."

PR Rule Number 2: Compromise, compromise, compromise.

"I don't know about that," he said. "But if I'm not inside you in the next sixty seconds, I'm going to lose my fucking mind. This is all I've thought about since I walked into your office. You in those goddamn snug skirts and fuck-me shoes. I wanted to take you on the desk right then and there. I wanted you to scream my name so all the little pricks in the office would know you were off-limits. I wanted to violate you in ways I can't even say out loud."

"So, what are you waiting for?" she asked.

He didn't answer with words. Instead, he slowly backed her up against the wall.

Chapter Eight

Let's face it, Jarod was not known for his couth or manners. A fact his family pointed out almost daily.

And here he was again, taking this reserved girl—who planned everything from the most mundane detail of her work to her coordinating bra-and-panty sets—headfirst into his depravity. In a fucking garage bathroom, no less. What the hell was with him and restrooms?

He lifted her up and set her on the edge of the counter near the sink. The space was small with a fairly high ceiling, and he worried the acoustics might present a problem. His concern was short-lived. The mirror, now directly behind Viv, offered a bonus view of her tempting ass, and he forgot about everything else. He gripped her soft, pliant thighs and opened her to him. His cock nestled dangerously close to her warm heat.

They were just a few layers of cotton from ecstasy.

"Jarod," she said when he rocked into her.

"Yes?" he asked, enjoying the friction between her legs.

The air was thick and sticky. Perspiration dotted his brow and arms. Vi wasn't immune. He felt the dampness behind her knees, and it fucking messed with his head.

"More," she gasped. "Please."

He pushed into her harder. Faster.

She moved with him, in tandem, and it was like the timing belt inside his head snapped. He couldn't think straight, and he didn't care where they were at this point. He had to have her. Gripping her thighs, Jarod pulled her impossibly close to him.

"If you would've told me two days ago I'd be spending the holiday like this, I would've said you were insane," Vi said between ragged breaths.

He was too overcome with need to keep up with conversation. His hunger for her wet heat and sweet musky smell made him ache. With two fingers, he pushed her panties to the side and buried them with a quick pump of his wrist.

"Two days ago, I wouldn't have believed I would be hitting your body like an addict," he finally answered.

Now that he'd found his target, his breathing slowed.

"Who would've thought?" she said.

"Thought what?" he asked. He fucking loved that she liked to talk while he got her off.

"Someone like me with someone like you."

It took him a moment to unscramble her words. Once he did, it killed the mood faster than a knee to the nuts. Slowly, he pulled away from her.

There it was. The truth staring him in the face. She didn't respect this place, the sport, or him. He was simply a job to her. Nothing more. She was using him to get to her next stop.

He'd been through that more times than he cared to count. This was a wall between them he couldn't break down. He wished he could be the kind of guy to blow it off. But hell if it didn't bug the shit out of him that she thought his profession was a joke. Thought he was a joke.

After all of it. The way he let her in. Shared this place with her. She must think he was some pathetic idiot.

"And there we have it," he said, taking a step back.

"Don't stop," she sobbed, confusion washed over her face.

He looked away and put the needed distance between them.

"What just happened?" she asked.

"I don't want to be the guy you go slumming with, Vi," he said.

"Slumming with?" Her eyebrows pressed together. "What the hell are you talking about? You have more money than God."

"I may not have a college degree, but I know what you were insinuating. *Someone like you with someone like me.* I'm not an idiot."

"I think you might be," she said, her face flushed and her words clipped. Two traits Jarod found incredibly arousing. Even in his pissed-off state.

"Look," he said. "I need to get back to the guys and the cars. I have a lot to do before I make the drive home."

"Okay," Vi said, her voice cracking as she slid off the counter and reached for her clothes. "Whatever you want. You're the client. But if you're up for *slumming it* later, I'll be at my apartment." She took his phone from the back pocket of his fire suit and typed in her address. "It's probably not the luxury you're used to, but you can see the fireworks from my front stoop."

• • •

Vi left the garage, and Jarod helped the guys put everything away, feeling like an asshole over the way he treated her.

Even worse was the way she didn't go on the attack after his psychotic behavior in the bathroom. Why?

And how could he get pissed about her take on him when that's all he'd shown her? The lewd jokes, the video, her closet, the bathroom. He let her believe the very worst in him, because he believed it. He could never measure up to his dad. So why not take the easy way out? Become a fuckup instead?

Trouble was, he had too much riding on things now. Everything mattered, and for the first time in his life, he cared. About what people thought about him, about his image, his ranking, and more and more, he found himself caring what *she thought.*

That's what had him driving like hell on wheels to Viv's apartment before she decided to go out without him. He'd apologize, just to calm the waters. She was going to be staying at his house starting tomorrow thanks to Henry or Miranda, or his fucking sponsors. He never did get the name behind the brainchild. But he was used to being in the dark about most decisions in his life. Regardless, he and Viv were going to be way too close to be fighting against all this shit. He needed her on his side.

Hell, he wanted her there.

Chapter Nine

Viv cranked up the air conditioner in her little Passat, trying to cool off on the drive home. It was working like shit. The air coming from the vent was warm, so she rolled down the window for some relief. It wasn't much better; the breeze was thick and heavy.

Good thing her lease was almost up. She was ready for a new car anyway, maybe something with a little more guts this time. Thanks to her new assignment, she was starting to understand the appeal of fast cars…and faster men.

Jarod Cage was working his way in. Her eyes kept flipping up to the rearview mirror, hoping she'd see him. Wishing he were following her home.

Why she wanted to see him of all people was asinine. He was moody, judgmental, and insulting. Her mind raced over the scene at the track—the events of the day, the way he showed her around and took her on the speedway in his car, everything that led up to the bathroom, and how he turned so cold on her. But worse? The way his face dropped at her words, hurt.

Shit, she needed to apologize.

That damn mouth of hers always got her into trouble. She replayed their conversation over and over again. It wasn't hard to see how he mistook her words. She saw it in his face when he pulled away from her.

The logical part of her brain said *it's done now.* She should just let it be. It was a terrible idea to get involved with a client—especially with so much on the line, for both of them. And as much as her body wanted him here with her, her head hoped he was in South Carolina by now. She'd have to face him soon enough, anyway.

But then she had to go and give him an open invitation. *You can see the fireworks from my front stoop.* Not that he'd take her up on it. He was pissed.

Viv entered her town house and took a quick shower, though she hated to wash away his scent, and wrapped up in her robe before she began packing for the weekend. According the itinerary Henry sent her, they'd stay overnight at Jarod's home tomorrow and prepare for the upcoming racing interviews she had set up between the races. She had a feeling he wasn't going to be too keen on that. The following day, they'd fly to Indiana.

She was going to have to find some way to apologize.

Viv's phone buzzed, and she ripped her bag apart trying to locate it, hoping it was Jarod on the end of the line.

"Happy Fourth of July," Mel yelled over what sounded like a jumping party.

"Hey, you," Viv said. "How's the party?"

"It'd be better if you were here." Her voice was a full

octave higher than normal, which meant she was two drinks away from a hangover. "Come for the fireworks, Vivi."

"I can't," she said. "I just got home from the most exhausting day." She paced from one end of her room to the other, stopping to straighten the throw pillows at the head of the bed.

"How's our horny race car driver?" Mel asked, like she needed any more reminders of the man who left her hanging just a few hours earlier.

"Hmm, let's just say I've had an easier time with clients." Viv went to her closet and decided on a new outfit for tomorrow. She was still a bundle of nervous energy. The shower did little to settle her mind. Or libido.

Could women get blue balls?

"Oh shit, did you get Caged?" Mel giggled and Viv sulked.

I wish.

"No," she said, dropping to her bed. "But what if I told you I wanted to?"

"I'd say yes," Mel squealed. "Yes. Yes. Hell yes."

"Of course you would," Viv said.

"I know I'm a little tipsy right now." Mel hiccupped. "But I promise you, this is a very good idea. You deserve this."

"I'm starting to think you're right," Viv said honestly, knowing Mel probably wouldn't remember their conversation in the morning.

"Of course I'm right," she said over the crowd. "Shit, Viv, looks like everyone's getting ready to go on the roof. Do me a favor, do yourself a favor, and get a piece of that hot-as-hell speed demon."

Viv worried she'd blown her chance.

Not two minutes later, she heard a loud engine rumble

outside. A glance out her window showed the man himself walking up her steps.

Don't mess it up, Viv.

She hauled ass down the stairs and almost fell in the process. Then she took a breath, smoothed down her hair, and reached for the doorknob.

"I'm sorry," they said at the same time when she opened the door.

Viv closed her eyes, holding back tears. She was becoming an emotional wreck. "I'm so glad you're here," she said, guiding him inside.

"Why are *you* sorry?" he asked. He'd changed out of his fire suit since she last saw him at the track, and was now wearing his jeans and a gray T-shirt. He never looked more appetizing.

"Ever since I left, I've replayed my words over and over again," she said. "Something I have to do constantly around you. I don't know why I say the things I do. But I get how it must've sounded to you when we were in the bathroom. It's not what I meant. Not at all."

She led him into the living room and motioned for him to have a seat.

"It doesn't matter." He patted the leather upholstery next to him, and she happily joined him. "Even if you did think I was beneath you, I should understand. I haven't given you a reason to think otherwise. Do we just bring out the worst in each other, or what?"

Viv thought about that for a moment. "No, not the worst. Maybe we just bring out parts of each other we're not used to showing the world. Today, I had the chance to see such a different part of you. And of racing. You have to know, I would never insult what you do or who you are."

"I'm happy to hear that." He smiled, and the weight of the day instantly lifted, leaving her feeling light. Almost euphoric.

"Well," she continued, apparently unable to leave well enough alone. "Except when you're acting like an ass. In that case, I just have to tell it like it is. Kinda my job."

"Just a suggestion," he said, running a hand through his hair. "It might be best to stick with *I'm sorry* next time. That speech right there was an unapology."

"Just being honest," she said. "No more shit, isn't that how you want it?"

"Right," he said. "But the reason I'm here is because I want to apologize to you. I acted like an oversensitive ass."

She didn't care about his apology, and more than anything, she didn't want to ruin the moment with words.

"No more talking," she ordered. It was time for action. "I'd like to finish what we started at the track."

"Oh no." He tugged on her hair. "You're not going to start bossing me around again, are you? I admit, there's a small part of me that finds it appealing—especially when you're wearing next to nothing, and propositioning me—but there are two places where I can't take orders."

Her nipples beaded under the soft cotton of her robe, and she bit the inside of her cheek to hold in a moan. She couldn't move too fast. This give-and-take thing they had going was fragile.

Slow and easy, Viv.

"Where won't you take orders?" she asked.

"In the car and in the bedroom," he said, and her stomach did little somersaults.

"Good thing we're not in the bedroom," she said on a dare, pushing him back against the sofa. She knelt over him, her fingertips grazing his scorching skin as she slid his shirt over his head. Damn, she wanted the Jarod Cage experience, and she wanted it now.

She'd spent enough time poking at him throughout the day to know his chest was as hard as granite. It was nothing compared to how it looked. The shirtless Cage was something dreams were made of. Muscular, but not bulky, the contours of his body were lean and taut. Light hair dusted his chest and led the way to his happy trail. A trip she wanted to make very soon.

The edge of his tattoo peeked out from the waistband of his jeans. She would be inspecting that as well.

"You can at least offer me a drink before you eye-fuck me," Jarod said in her ear, his stubble tickling her neck, bringing a welcome coolness to the heat. "Warm a guy up, for Christ's sake."

"I've seen the way you work," she said, straddling his lap. "No foreplay needed. In the car or in the bedroom. Or the bathroom, closet, garage…"

He pulled her closer, grinding against her sweet spot, further proving her point. She was instantly overcome by his strength, his warmth. His citrus scent was mixed with cedar and spice, and it was absolutely intoxicating. She wanted to bathe in Eau de Cage.

"Bed," he growled. "Now."

Her senses flooded with the strength of his body pushing up against hers, his rough voice, making demands in her ear.

"I didn't take you for a traditionalist." She moved off his lap and stood, reaching for his hand.

"I'm doing it right this time." He laced his fingers in hers and followed her up the stairs. God, she wanted him.

"Fine." She shuddered. "I can work with a bed." Her stomach had moved on to front handsprings by this point. She was really going to do this.

"It's okay, baby," he said, as if he could feel the turmoil in her body. "I won't do anything you don't want to do."

She knew it didn't matter. One touch, one look, one word, and he'd have her on the edge.

"Nice place," he said, looking down at her townhome from the open staircase, as if trying to ease her nerves.

"It's temporary," she said. A sentiment that seemed to close her off more than open her up lately.

"Of course," Jarod said in a tone she'd never heard him use. "Next stop: New York."

Once they made it up to her loft, Jarod whistled. "So this is where the magic happens?"

"I guess we'll see," she said.

"Don't tell me." He checked out the spotless room. "You haven't christened the place yet?"

"I just moved here," she said in defense.

"Yes, like two years ago. I read your Elite bio." He walked around her room—a space that was night and day different from the main floor of her townhome and her office. This room actually had sprinkles of Viv in it. She watched his face light up with interest as he took it all in.

It was here where she was most comfortable in her skin. She had feminine touches of flowers, and lace, and soft material. Romantic furniture, rather than the sleek modern stuff in the other rooms. Photos of her family, books, and old paintings that resembled Monet and Rembrandt.

"About that drink," she said, half joking, half hoping for

a quick delay so she could settle down.

"We both know *I* don't need a drink." He turned toward her and brushed her wet hair off her shoulders.

"What *do* you need?" Viv asked.

"A kiss," he said in that low, raspy voice, before untying her robe.

"That all?" She enjoyed pushing him, and more than that, she loved to listen to his voice.

"Hell no, but that's where we'll start." His fingertips skimmed along her waist, and she quivered.

A kiss? No, no, no. A kiss was too intimate. She'd learned that in the closet. She sucked on her lower lip, imagining his lips on hers. No, she just wanted the release.

"We don't need to mess around with that," she said, convinced she didn't need all the pomp and circumstance. Just a quick wham, bam, thank you, ma'am, would do quite nicely. Thank you very much.

He had other ideas.

Jarod walked her backward toward the bed. He was so close she could almost taste the mint on his breath. He used his thumb to pull her lip from her teeth, preparing her.

He crowded her space, but she didn't feel claustrophobic. She felt more free than she could ever remember feeling. And when he slanted his lips down over hers and made her open for him, she couldn't get close enough.

His tongue explored her mouth so thoroughly—it felt like deliciously crushed velvet. Viv was light-headed from the lack of oxygen, so she held on, knowing he wouldn't let her fall. He cradled her head as he pulled her bottom lip into his hot mouth and sucked like he was trying to punish her for putting him in such a state. He mapped every part of her mouth. He was taunting, hungry, relentless.

Viv didn't deny him.

It was the kind of kiss she'd only read about in books. The kind she only watched on her racy cable TV shows. It wasn't sweet or romantic. This was no old-fashioned Hollywood dip. No heel lifting off the floor in a precious little bend. It was deep. His lips taking, tongue delving, mouth moving until every inch of her felt infused with him.

He didn't let up until she was a boneless puddle of lust.

"I don't," Viv started to say when she came up for air.

"Don't what?" Jarod stilled, concern washing over his face.

"I don't want to be another notch on your steering wheel." Viv tried for lighthearted, but worried she came off pathetic. Still, she was terrified that if she went *there* with Jarod, she'd never come back from it intact. Especially after that all-consuming kiss. But she also knew she couldn't go on like this, her body betraying her whenever he was near. They'd just have to keep it…dirty. No pesky emotions allowed.

"It wouldn't be like that with you," he said. "We have an arrangement. Strictly business. Because let's face it. We need each other. The only way we're going to get through it is to get it out of our system."

She nodded, understanding him completely.

"I can't stop thinking about you," he whispered. "Your smell, your goddamn lips, and all that silky hair. I want to wrap it around my fist and tug—hold you in place so I can do what I want to you. I want to see you. Worship you. Fuck you until we can't move. One night. It'll do us both a world of good. We can't go on like this. My cock aches, baby. I can't think straight."

Viv knew the feeling.

His breathing was heavy, and it seemed to bounce off the walls. Each movement—the shift of feet on the floor, the wet sounds of their kisses, his deep, dirty words—were magnified in the open space.

Her fingers dived into his hair, unable to hold back as need pulled low in her belly and filthy desires filled her head. He was right; it was past time to take care of this distraction. If they didn't, it would ruin them both.

Jarod held her, as if they were dancing, and answered her silent plea by pushing a knee between her legs, letting her rock into him. "Better?" he asked.

"Not good enough," she answered. He was making this too intimate.

To that, he pulled back and gripped her hips in his hands. She gasped, and his knee rose higher. Harder. The pressure was exquisite, but she wanted more.

"Really?" he said in challenge. "What would be enough for you, greedy girl?" He peppered her neck with kisses that put her so out of sorts, she started to panic a little.

"Stop teasing," she said in frustration. "If we're going to get this out of our system, let's fucking do it already."

Viv was never the aggressor in bed. Never had been. Never really needed to be. But this man got under her skin in so many ways. Just for once, she wanted him to listen to her.

"Can't we ever have things my way?" she asked.

"No," Jarod said, removing his knee. "We can't. I'm not one of those needle-dick admirers you're used to."

"What are you talking about?"

"I've got your number, babe. I've seen your type before."

She was worried he was comparing her to Gina. For some unexplainable reason, that pissed her right off.

"I'm not a type, you asshole. I'm a woman," She pounded on his chest. "A woman who doesn't want to be messed with."

"Afraid you might lose control with me, Vi?"

Her eye twitched.

"That's it, isn't it?" he said. "First, it's all business. Then, when it suits you, you use that tight little body to tease the piss out of me. All fun and games in public. You loved it in the fucking garage or closet where things couldn't get too crazy—just a quick rub to make you come. But you only wanted it when you had an easy out. What about here, Vi? There's no one to stop us."

"Stop talking," she pleaded, but made no move to flee.

He listened. Blessed all, he finally listened. She swallowed and let her head clear. She needed to think, gain some flipping composure.

As she did, his eyes warmed. He actually looked sympathetic.

Though only for a moment.

That warm expression heated. Darker. Darker.

"Okay," he said, though nothing was remotely okay. For either of them. He smoothed her hair.

And then wrapped a fist in it and pulled. With her head tipped back, he had perfect access to her ear. To continue with the debauchery she was growing to love.

"You're right. The teasing stops now."

She bit back a curse, and apprehension melted away.

"And the fucking starts."

Viv lifted her chin, pretending his words didn't just turn her inside out. "That's all I've been asking for."

She was ready, and damn it to hell, she wanted to see the prize this time. No, she wanted to touch and taste and take her fill of it. He'd touched her body on three separate encounters—yes, she was counting—and not once did she get to explore his. She planned to change that, pronto.

Viv pulled him over to the edge of her bed and took a seat as he stood before her. It was the perfect exploring position, and she wasted no time flicking open the button of his jeans. She palmed him over the denim and stroked—once, twice—before opening his fly for the surprise of a lifetime.

His cock sprang from his pants. No boxers or briefs to hold him back. He was there for the taking, every thick inch of him. In the dim light, she could make out that black mark from the video. It was a number on the side of his thigh. It sparked her curiosity, but right now she had more pressing priorities.

Her hands itched to touch him, hold him, and when they finally did, he was so hard it made her soak right through her panties. Jarod locked his hands over hers, over his throbbing erection.

She gripped him hard and moved her hand up, down, and over his impressive length. He slowly handed over his control, and she took it happily. Stripping him of the rest of his clothes, she finally had him where she wanted him.

Pulling him down on the bed, she covered his body with hers—skin on skin. Full of currents and heat, igniting until she was ready to explode.

Jarod gripped her ass and tortured her with the tip of his cock before flipping her over—stripping the last bits of lace that covered her. Then he reached for his pants on the floor and produced a condom in record time.

Yes. God yes.

She was swollen and achy, and the sweet slide into pleasure couldn't come fast enough.

"Please," she said for the second time today, making her so incredibly needy.

Jarod nestled into her center, his cock grazing her opening.

Her legs fell to the side shamelessly as she made room for him. He stretched and filled her as he plunged into her aching warm heat.

The pressure and friction were mind-blowing. She was speechless, but the voice in her mind was painfully clear. More. Don't stop. God, yes. "Take anything you want."

"Anything?" he growled. Apparently her last wish was said aloud.

She nodded in reply to his question, and he continued his assault. She would give him anything he wanted, and she'd do it happily.

The delayed gratification from his earlier torture had her pleasure points unbearably sensitive. Each touch, each lick, each stroke left her teetering on the edge.

Then a tightening low in her belly began. She almost didn't recognize the sensation, it had been so long.

"Ah," Jarod groaned. "That's it." He thrust so painfully deep. "You're so damn tight."

Her nipples stung as they rubbed against his chest. Her eyes rolled back in her head. He didn't stop pounding into her, again and again.

"Come for me, baby. I've got you."

She moved hard and fast toward her climax. An overload of pleasure took over, and soon she was gasping for air.

But Jarod didn't relent. He fucked her so hard, the springs in the mattress threatened to break.

Then, with one final, punishing push, they fell over the edge.

Chapter Ten

Vivian Blake was the most amazing thing he'd ever seen. Lying under him with her hair fanned out on the pillow, her forehead glistening, her lips in midsigh.

And that was saying a lot, because he'd seen a few things in his day. Though despite his reputation and that damn tape, he wasn't the sex-craved monster the media made him out to be. Yes, of course, he'd had his share. And if you asked most of the women he had been with, they'd probably say he was dirty as hell. Still, he didn't have dozens of women scratched into his steering wheel, as Viv put it.

Truth was, the act—the bad-boy image—helped hide who he really was. If he could distract with dirty words and a well-timed slap to the ass, he didn't really have to connect or feel. That's all the women wanted from him anyway. The experience—the thought of him—but not the real man.

Viv was already different. And that's why he had to get the hell out of here.

He dropped his arm over the side, snatching his jeans.

"Can you stay and hold me a minute?" she asked, making Jarod feel like the world's biggest dick. She shouldn't have to ask.

"I'm sorry," she said after a long silence. "It's okay. You have a long drive."

"No, I can stay," he said, stunned that the next thing that rolled out of his mouth was the absolute truth. "I want to stay."

He pulled the comforter over their naked bodies and shifted her into the crook of his arm so she could use his shoulder as a pillow.

"Tell me about your tattoo," she said. "Is it a racing number?"

"Yeah, it is," he said. "My dad's."

Jarod didn't like to talk about it, but Vi had dug her way in so deep, it didn't really hurt to let her in further.

"I know it's in a weird place, on the side of my hip, but I don't like it visible to anyone."

"Why?" she asked.

He wasn't sure how to put it into words, but he owed her to try. "When he was alive, we had very few private moments. I resented that for so long that I wasn't going to share his death with anyone. The press think I'm indifferent, especially when I race on the same track that took my father's life. They want my sob story, but I'm not going to give it to them. And I don't give a shit what they say about it. I race and that's it."

"This is one time where I agree with you," she said, taking his hand.

"Thanks for shutting down the questions about my dad

today," he said, realizing that maybe she understood more than she let on.

"I think it's despicable that anyone would even bring him up. I'm so sorry you've had to go through that. But I will teach you how to handle the media. I promise."

They stayed like that for a long time, holding each other. He wasn't sure who needed it more.

Vi's breathing slowed, and Jarod's heartbeat did as well, matching hers. They hadn't known each other for a week. Yet she felt so right in his arms. Almost as good as he felt between her legs.

Typically, sex was all he needed to calm his nerves. With Vi, he didn't feel sated. Not even close with her there in his arms.

Just a few more minutes. He'd indulge in her warmth, savor the floral scent wafting from her in a delicious cloud, and let himself have this for just a few more minutes.

Shit, he was in so much trouble. If he couldn't handle this, what the hell was he going to do when she was under his roof? He liked the sound of that far too much.

But he wouldn't think about that until he had to. For now, he'd concentrate on her breathing.

She rolled closer in her sleep. He loved the way her body reacted to him, especially when she turned her brain off. She wrapped an arm around him, and he settled in. And before he knew it, his exhaustion took him under.

• • •

Jarod was outside in his yard when Viv arrived in Cotton Creek the next day, not that he was waiting on her or anything.

He'd moved all the vehicles out of his driveway to make room for her, and had Mrs. B make up some fresh lemonade and cookies.

All he had to do now was have Mrs. B help locate his balls, because he lost them somewhere between Atlanta and home.

Viv puttered in, driving her clown car. It made him uneasy. He'd rather see her in something bigger, an SUV or something a little more substantial. He was about to raise the issue, but when she got out of the car, the girl was a drippy mess.

"What the heck, Vi?" he asked, rushing up to the car to take her bag off her shoulder. "Get caught in a rainstorm?"

"It's my stupid car," she said, blowing her bangs off her forehead. "And the stupid air-conditioning."

"Conked out on ya, huh?"

"My lease is up next month, so I'm just going to try to hold out until then. I don't want to put money into something I'm not going to keep, ya know?"

"Sure," he said. "Just temporary." He was beginning to hate that phrase. "But you can't drive around Atlanta without air. I'll take a look at it before we head out."

"No," she said, batting him away. "You're not fixing my car when you have one of the most important races of your life in a few days."

"Geez, cut the drama." He laughed. "I'm nervous enough as it is."

"I doubt that. By the way, thanks for staying last night."

"I was happy to," he said.

"Look." She gnawed on the inside of her cheek in that

adorable way of hers. "I don't want you to worry. I know it was just a onetime thing."

Jarod considered her, remembering how difficult it was to leave in the morning, and wondered if she really believed the bullshit she was spewing.

Because he sure didn't.

She might have been a little soggy, but she still looked absolutely edible. Her hair was held back in a soft braid that hung over her shoulder, and she wore no makeup, which made her look much younger than her twenty-six years. Her jeans—shit, the jeans—were almost worse than the dress she wore the day before. Snug in all the right places.

"It's okay," he said. "I'm not expecting any sexual favors from you while you're here."

"I didn't mean—"

"I'm just playing." He bumped a shoulder into hers. "Let's get you a room and, don't take this the wrong way, a shower. I'm going to see what we can do about the *stupid car.*"

• • •

The woman was meticulous with her clothes, her work, her apartment. But her car? A fucking disaster. He'd spent the last two hours fixing the air conditioner, changing her oil and filters, and replacing spark plugs.

"Vi," he called when he walked into the den. "We need to have a little chat about basic car maintenance."

The woman paid him no mind as she worked away. She'd changed into a tiny pair of shorts and a tank top and sat right there on his couch—her papers, computer, and gadgets taking up residence on his coffee table. He forgot for a moment why he came blazing in.

"I know, I know," she dismissed him. "It's just a lease, so don't worry."

"I'm not worried," he said to the top of her head. "I fixed the mess."

"You did?" She put down her gadgets and glanced up with a surprised look on her face. "You know how to do all that stuff?"

"Are you trying to deliberately hurt me?" he asked with a hand to his heart.

"No." She smiled. "I would just assume your crew does that stuff for you."

"Hey, I like to get my hands dirty once in a while."

"Yes, I believe I know what you mean," she said. "Thanks for fixing my air conditioner. My hair will be thanking you on the way home on Sunday."

"You're welcome." He took a seat next to her. "So what's all this?"

"Well, I was thinking we could start our prep by going over some of your rockier interviews—"

"What?" He feigned shock. "I have rocky interviews?"

"What I'd like to know is who was helping you before I came along? Because they should be fired, and never be allowed to practice PR again."

"I didn't work much with the handlers at the races," he admitted.

"You don't say," Viv scoffed.

"Let's get it over with, then," he said, waving her on.

She tapped a finger to the remote, and the screen flashed to life. "This is Daytona, I believe."

"Oh, great, this is the one where I was trailing Wooly and gave him a bump. And he ended up spinning out. Wait, why are you fast-forwarding this?"

"Because you're fine on the track. You make big moves when you need to, but you're not reckless or a poor sport. Everyone has a lot of respect for you out there. But here"—she signaled to the TV—"when you were presented with the trophy, you're a mess. This is where I can help you."

"This was months ago and had nothing to do with the predicament."

"Oh really? Why do you think these guys are having a field day with you?"

"Because they're assholes?"

"That may be so, but so are you, mister. Exhibit A." Viv turned up the volume on the interview after the race.

"Great job today at Bristol. You won."

"Yep, that's what they say."

She paused the tape. "Right there, dick move."

"Well, he's a dick reporter. How am I supposed to respond to that?"

"He's just fishing for a good sound bite. How about say 'thank you' and talk about why you're thrilled to win at a track like Bristol. Talk about history, talk about the race, your teammates. Anything. Give them something."

"I think I've given them plenty." He kicked up his feet on the table. "Why are you so high on the media, anyway?"

"I'm not high on them. I just understand them. That's part of my job." Viv hit fast-forward to cue up the next video. "So see, what he's trying to do in this interview is—"

"I know," Jarod interrupts. "Brooks Fenn has been following me for my career, I know exactly what he was trying to do in that clip. And I know because he's an asshole."

"Next tape," Viv continued.

They watched the screen as Jarod took his prize and kissed the trophy girl in a way that required an FCC censor.

"It was a distraction technique," he said, sheepishly.

He didn't miss the way Viv was squirming in her seat. "Well, it made you look like a complete douche bag," she snapped.

"Anything else?" He tried to hide his smirk.

"Yes, there's plenty, actually."

• • •

After what felt like hours of media training, Jarod had officially agreed to Operation: Make Nice with the Press.

They concluded with his first phone interview after the bar bathroom incident.

"That was hell," Jarod said after they finished.

"Eating crow usually is," Viv said.

Jarod turned on *SportsCenter* after their lesson, trying to catch the commentary for the upcoming race.

"Hungry?" he asked Viv as she continued to work.

"Don't tell me you cook, too?" she asked.

"Mrs. B made up some stuff. I just have to heat it up."

"Who's Mrs. B?"

"My mama's friend. She cooks and helps me take care of the house, and her husband, Dally, looks over my toys outside and keeps an eye on the place when I'm gone."

"I wondered about that. You must have a killer security system."

"Well, Dally is a former army sergeant, so he has this

place locked down like Fort Knox. But I'm not too concerned. This is Cotton Creek—everyone knows everyone and their people. I'm not worried about them. The jackwads from out of town? Maybe. Especially as the season kicks up. But the people here are very protective—nobody would give out any information on my property."

"That sounds a little too trusting for the Jarod Cage I know," Viv said.

"Maybe, but a guy can't be looking over his shoulder all the time, right?"

Chapter Eleven

Jarod Cage's place was the polar opposite of Viv's. With the exception of her bedroom.

He had family portraits, awards, artifacts from his travel, art, all over the place. And the books? Holy heck, the books. Classics and mysteries, tons of biographies and nonfiction accounts of almost every American war in history. He had his own freaking library.

She poked around while he went to the kitchen to warm up their dinner. There was nothing temporary about this place. She envied him that.

He brought out some wine—a very nice Pinot, Viv noted—and paired it with some kind of shrimp dish and biscuits. Viv felt her butt expanding just looking at it.

Jarod set it all down in front of her.

"That looks amazing," she said, inhaling the spicy scent of the shrimp. "What is it?"

"This?" Jarod looked confused. "You've never had

shrimp and grits before?"

"Sorry, no."

"Oh, my poor deprived little Yank. This is the ultimate comfort food. I usually have it for breakfast, but it works anytime. It's insane with the wine. Mrs. B always makes up a batch for me during the season. It's my ritual the night before we head out. Once we're on the road, I try to eat pretty clean, and I don't drink. But the night before is like goddamn Mardi Gras."

"Just keep in mind not all of us are getting behind the wheel and shedding weight," she warned. "I read that you lose close to ten pounds during each race."

"My record is seventeen. Then again, I have a lot more nervous energy than most. And I hardly think you have anything to worry about."

Jarod dished up their servings. He took a huge scoop from Viv's bowl and put it up to her lips.

He was right. It was comfort food with a warm, spicy blanket of flavor that had her shoveling it in hand over fist.

Jarod ate slowly, taking in the highlights from last year's race, and she watched with increased interest as the drama unfolded on the track.

The number six car was trailing the number five, bumping it from behind. The five straightened out and started to pull away. Jarod groaned, and she felt a little ache in her stomach. This was his life, and it was scary as heck.

The six moved a lane over and inched up toward the five, until it could ride it into the wall. Sparks flew everywhere, and a few other cars got caught up in it all. The six car cut off the number five, causing him to spin out. His rear end was hit by one of the passing cars. The ambulance raced to the side of the track. Number six sped away, while the five sat there totaled.

The driver got out of the car, limping pretty badly. It was a miracle he could walk.

"Whoa," Viv said.

"No shit," Jarod agreed. "It was a rough day at the track."

The video cut to a shot of a beautiful brunette storming up to the platform of the racers' wives.

"What's going on here?" Viv asked.

"That's Tammy," Jarod said, pointing to the brunette. "Ronny's wife. She's going to confront Sixpack's wife, Emily."

"Why?"

"Because her dumbass husband is being reckless as shit."

"Oh my God." Viv giggled. "So she's going all Patsy on him?"

"What are you talking about?"

Viv belted out her best rendition of "Stand by Your Man."

"Wow." Jarod looked at her with disgust.

"What?"

"Well, for one, that song is by Tammy Wynette," he said. "And two, you really don't get it, do you?"

"Don't get in a huff, I'm just goofing around," she said, but she got the sick feeling she'd put her damn foot in her mouth again.

"Sorry, but this isn't the kind of shit you make fun of. That asshole put Ronny's life in danger. Tammy and Ronny have three little boys—all who were there watching this unfold. You better believe Tammy's not going to let it go. The wives have a lot of influence and power on the circuit.

Tammy told Emily to get her *man* to calm the fuck down so he doesn't kill somebody out there. She was protecting her family, Vi."

She felt like a real dumbass. Again. This was becoming a problem. Jarod Cage seemed to bring out the absolute worst in her.

Jarod didn't hold Viv's comments over her head. He, in fact, held nothing, and Viv went to bed starved for his touch.

• • •

"To get to this track, we fly right into the infield," Jarod said on their way to his sponsor's hangar in the morning. They would be taking off from the small airport in North Carolina, which made Viv a little nervous. Wasn't it always the small planes that went down? But wait, a plane couldn't land in the infield, could it?

Jarod seemed to understand her confusion when he looked over. "We fly in a chopper," he said.

"Ah." She nodded, feeling a bit like a fool. Viv tried to wrap her head around it all. "Geez, it's so *West Wing*."

"*West Wing*?" he asked. "Wasn't that show a little before your time?"

"Probably," she said. "I haven't had time to watch much TV in the last decade, but occasionally I watch reruns late at night when I can't sleep."

"I should call you C.J., then," he said. "Wasn't she the PR gal?"

"She was."

"Well, C.J., believe it or not, none of this is for show," he said. "The airport is just too far away from the track."

"Shoot. That's where I booked my hotel."

"Hotel?" His eyebrows pulled together in a way that made Viv want to smooth them out with her finger. Or her tongue.

"Yes," she said. "I should've asked the best place to stay. That's okay, I'll find something closer." She started frantically typing on her phone.

"The best place to stay is with me," Jarod said.

"In your motor home?" She could feel her cheeks turning pink.

"I have plenty of room," he said. "Actually, I thought Miranda and Henry already had it all worked out. They've orchestrated everything else to ensure I don't have a second to get into trouble."

"Right," she said. "That's why I'm not so sure that's a good idea."

"Why? Still thinking about the other night?"

"No," she lied. "I'm good. You were right, we got it out of our system."

"Right." He smirked. "Just like I said we would. So stay with me."

The way he said it was tender and dirty all at the same time. She was sure he'd gotten his fill of her, but she didn't think she'd ever get enough of him. Still, he was the client, and she needed to keep him happy. Plus, if she booked the hotel room now, it'd be the equivalent of saying she still wanted him. And then he'd be even more of a nightmare to deal with.

"You're sure there's enough room?" Viv asked again, trying to keep the mood light.

"Absolutely," he said. "It'll be easier that way, and save

you time. I'm sure you have other things to do besides babysit me."

"Now that you mention it," she said, "I do have to wrap up a few other cases over the next few days. That way, I'll be all yours by the time the race starts."

"It's settled then," he said, while she tried to get her bearings. It was a futile effort considering she was riding with him in his Lamborghini at that very moment. Silver and sleek, Viv was sure it cost more than several years of her salary at Elite.

"I can't believe you're going to leave this at the hangar," she said.

"They have a special garage for my baby, don't worry. I know it's a little showy, but driving this thing pumps me up before a race weekend and is something to look forward to driving home."

The car was ridiculous, but what really took her breath away was the way he drove it. Those damn arms got her every time. The way he shifted and handled the steering wheel. It made her positively melty.

Jarod drove them to the airport, and when they arrived, he escorted her to their waiting chopper. Viv had ridden in one once before, when she was interning at the local TV station, so she knew to duck as they walked to load up. She also knew how the headsets worked, so at least she wouldn't look like a total rookie. All PR majors had to get experience working in media as well. The old "know thy enemy" philosophy. Actually, Viv usually found the media to be more of a help than a detriment, and she intended on using them to put Jarod's reputation back in the good graces of the public.

PR Rule Number 18: Use each and every tool in your

toolbox.

Jarod helped lift her inside, and the two of them settled in the backseat. The pilot pointed to the headsets, and they put them on.

"Nice to see you again, Mr. Cage." The pilot, who looked to be in his late fifties, turned in his seat and flashed a smile. Okay, at his age, he should have plenty of experience. No glasses; that was also a good sign. Viv strategically leaned in, sniffing for any signs of booze.

Hey, she was putting her life in his hands, so she had every right to check him out.

"You too, J.D.," Jarod said before making introductions. "This is Vivian Blake."

"Nice to meet you," she said.

"Likewise."

"How's it looking up there today?" Jarod asked.

"Beautiful," J.D. said. "It'll be a smooth ride, and we'll have you on the track in no time."

Viv took some deep breaths to calm down, but it wasn't helping. Her palms were wet, and she was trembling.

Jarod strapped in and Viv followed, but her hands were too shaky to get the buckle to cooperate.

"Hey." Jarod leaned over and moved her headset so he could talk to her privately. "Are you okay?" He pushed her hands away and took care of her seat belt himself.

"I'll be fine," she said. "I'm just a little nervous. I've flown before, so I'm not sure why I'm being such a baby."

"Give yourself a break," he said, taking her hand. "You've had a helluva few days. Just hold on to me. As long as I'm here, you have nothing to worry about."

She concentrated on his grip and the way his thumb

stroked her palm. It was soothing, and the panic began to subside.

"See, Vi," he said. "You're already doing better. We're going to take off now, so hold on."

She did, but that was the problem. She held on so tight, she was afraid she'd never want to let go.

• • •

The ride in the chopper was about an hour and a half up to Indiana. They soared above the track and then landed right in the infield like Jarod promised.

The sheer awe of it all didn't stop once they were on the ground, either. Viv had never seen anything like the racing spectacle. She'd been to some of the biggest sports venues on the planet, but this? It was different. There was so much activity, so many people hoping to catch a glimpse of their favorite driver, but at the same time, it was more personal. It felt homey? Was that the right word?

"Welcome to the circuit, baby," Jarod said, and he took their bags and led her toward a golf cart.

He loaded the bags in the back and fired up the cart, and they took off toward the driver lot. When they arrived to the sea of million-dollar motor homes, there was a buzz of activity. Young guys buffed and shined the huge homes on wheels. They put out area rugs, set up outdoor seating areas, and adjusted satellites on the rooftops.

Drivers socialized and consulted with members of their crew; the WAGs (wives and girlfriends) chatted with friends and watched over the children. And they were everywhere.

Jarod yucked it up with the other drivers, played with

the kids, and introduced Viv at every opportunity. The uneasiness from the night before had completely subsided. This was Jarod at his best. Until the media came around.

Once the camera was in his face, he grabbed Viv, jumped back on the golf cart, and hit the gas. He nearly took down the reporter in the process.

"Remember," she said, when they were out of yelling distance from the press. "You need to let them in. Let them get to know you."

"I will," he said. "Once we're settled. I promise to do as you say, but I still have to maintain some balance with them. Okay?"

"I guess that's fair," she allowed.

"This is it." He pulled the golf cart up to a black-and-silver luxury motor coach.

He called it his bus. But before she got a good look, they were interrupted by a guy speeding up to them on a tricked-out golf cart.

"Why are you slumming it down on this side of the lot, Cage?" a guy yelled, before squealing the brakes as he pulled up to Jarod. Wearing flannel and facial hair, he resembled a mountain man. A friendly mountain man. He looked to be in his late thirties, but it was difficult to tell what was under all the whiskers.

"You've got that all wrong," Jarod said to him with a smile. "The west side of the lot is reserved for all the riffraff. We're more selective here on the east."

"Is that so?" the man asked, before jumping off the cart and wrapping Jarod in a bear hug.

"Damn straight," Jarod said when he released him. "Viv Blake, this is my only threat on the track, Charlie Stewart."

Viv definitely recognized the name. She'd come across him a few times during her research.

"I'm also your only friend on the track." He laughed and extended a hand to Viv. "Nice to meet you, ma'am."

"Nice to meet you, too," she said.

"So how you holding up?" he asked Jarod, taking the turn for a more serious topic.

"You know me, I'm used to it," he said, and then went on to explain Viv's role and the new PR plan for Jarod Cage 2.0.

"Jesus," Charlie said. "If they had the Twitter and all that crap when I was coming up, shit, I'm not sure I'd still be here."

"It hasn't been easy." Jarod ran a hand through his hair.

"Hey now." Charlie rested his hands on Jarod's shoulders. "Everyone is entitled to a little bathroom boom-boom now and then. Don't beat yourself up over it." He wiggled his brows, and both Viv and Jarod laughed.

The two men caught up until Charlie got a text from his wife. Then he took off. Boy, she'd never seen anyone move so fast.

"Man, I thought he'd never leave." Jarod winked.

"He's a good friend of yours?" she asked.

"One of the best, actually," he said. "We've been together since the beginning, and he's had his own share of tough times, so you know, misery loves company and all that. But he's showing well this year. After me, of course."

"Of course," she teased.

"Come on." He led her to the door of the motor coach. "Let me show you around."

They walked in and Viv thought it was as nice as her townhome, with quite a few more personal touches. The *bus* had two bedrooms, an office, a kitchen, two bathrooms, and a living area. It was plush, and she didn't mind her new accommodations at all.

"You can take this room," Jarod said. "It has its own bathroom, so you'll have the privacy you need. Go ahead and relax. We got in early, and nothing really starts kicking for a few hours yet."

He dropped her bag on the bed in the large room, which also had a desk and a huge TV. Viv knew something was amiss, so she went out to take a look at the other room at the other end of the motor coach. When she took in the space, it was just as she thought—his was definitely the smaller of the two.

"I'm not taking your room," she said, joining him back in the master suite.

"How do you know this is my room?" he asked.

"This is the master," she said. "I'm not kicking you out of your room."

"You're not kicking me out," he said. "I'm giving it to you—even though I obviously belong in the *master* room for many reasons."

She hated the way her cheeks burned at his naughty words, but she was happy that things between them were back to normal again. Whatever *normal* was.

"I'm serious. You need the space. I want you comfortable and well-rested."

"The other bed is just as comfortable," he said, grabbing her hand and leading her into his suite. He pulled her onto the bed with him and she squealed. Yes, he was back to his playful self, and Viv was smitten.

Geez, did people even say that word anymore?

She couldn't help it—Jarod's Southern charm combined with his naughty alpha tendencies had her acting like a heroine in one of her old-fashioned romance novels. All blushing and uncertain, and, well, smitten.

Jarod turned on his side and pushed on the mattress. "See? Soft, right?"

"Right," she said with a grin.

"Plus, I don't need the desk or the privacy." He winked.

"Okay, you're the boss." She pushed up and off the bed. "I'll be lounging in my master suite if you need me." And with that, she went bouncing down the hallway into her new room.

PR Rule Number 4: Never argue with the client.

She unpacked her things, checked in with her mom and Mel, and started writing a press release for Jarod's expected win, to stay a step ahead. She was that confident. Or she was trying to be.

She had finished it by the time a woman's voice echoed in the other room.

Viv came out to the living space, where a young woman stopped by to give Jarod his schedule. She felt something she wasn't at all comfortable with.

"Hey, Vi," Jarod said. "This is my handler, Kelsey."

"Nice to meet you." Viv shook her hand, pretending not to be fazed by the lanky blond beauty standing before her. She then turned to Jarod, wanting to dismiss Kelsey. Like pronto. "I have some things I'd like to go over with you."

"I need to talk to my handler first," he said. "I'll be back shortly."

"But—" she stuttered.

"Relax," he said. "We have plenty of time. I won't be

gone long."

The two of them walked away, and she swore she saw Kelsey smirk. Viv felt a burning in her belly, and not the good kind. They looked far too cozy together. She just prayed he hadn't slept with her. Because as far as Viv was concerned, she was the only handler he needed.

• • •

Viv didn't make it out of the bus much over the weekend. She was working behind the scenes and only surfaced during Jarod's interviews, the qualifying races, and the big show.

The day of the big race, her computer dinged—for video chat—first thing in the morning. Viv opened the screen to Mel's sweet face.

"Hey, honey," Mel said. "Are you ready for today?"

"As I'll ever be." Viv pinched the bridge of her nose. "The question is, is Jarod ready?"

"Well, from this end, *both* of you are looking amazing. He killed it in the interviews on Friday, and your handiwork was in every word that came out of his mouth. Miranda's even let us keep the TVs on in the media room. Soph, Jess, and I are in there watching whenever we can. You're impressing the hell out of everyone."

She found that hard to believe. "Everyone?"

"Not Fredrick, of course," Mel said, scrunching up her nose. "Actually, he may have made some *suggestions* to Miranda."

"He *what*?" She hated not being there to keep an eye on him.

"I know. That fucker really dills my pickle," Mel said.

"Don't worry, though, the girls and I have your back. When he brought his *thoughts* up to Miranda, we basically discounted everything he said. So you just focus on your plan once your boy wins, and we'll handle things back here. Oh, and watch Jarod around Lach."

"Lachlan Walker?" Viv knew the name. He always placed high in the races with Jarod and a few other elite drivers, like Ronny and Charlie Stewart.

"That's him, the one and sexy," Mel purred. "He and Jarod don't mix, and you don't need a scuffle after all the great work you've been doing. But if you do run into that Aussie hunk of beef, you could always set me up."

"I thought you were waiting for *the one*," Viv joked. "I don't think your parents would be happy with a renegade race car driver."

"Plans have changed," Mel said. "They're on a matchmaking mission, so I need to start sowing my oats before they sell me off."

Viv always thought Mel was kidding when she said things like that, but lately she was beginning to wonder what kind of control Mel's parents really had over her relationships. But that was a conversation for another day. She thanked Mel and promised to do some recon on Lach's relationship status—even though she'd never met the guy. Then she went down to the garage to check on her troublemaker.

She only got within ten feet of Jarod down on pit road. People were waiting in line to talk to him, and Henry was having a rather animated discussion with him at the moment. Still, it didn't take Jarod too long to look up. It was as if he knew she was there.

He tipped his head in her direction and put his hands up.

She didn't want to bother him, so she gave a thumbs-up and mouthed, "Good luck."

Jarod smiled and nodded, and she left him in Henry's capable hands.

She took a little walk to calm her nerves. The energy at the track was tangible. Music blaring and people cheering, the stands were packed to capacity. Viv was documenting all of it with still photos and video clips. She had secured a few features for some of the racing blogs, so she was providing them with everything she could.

Any chance she could get to portray Jarod in a positive light, she was going to take. No job was too small at this point. This was going to be a flawless campaign. It was a little time-consuming, but she made it back to the bus by the time the announcer had the drivers starting their engines.

She watched the race on the rooftop of the bus, alone. She wasn't there to socialize, no matter how fun the WAGs made it look with wine and snacks. Plus, she was so nervous for Jarod, she wouldn't have been able to enjoy herself no matter how hard she tried. Each point meant everything to him at this stage of the competition if he hoped to make it to the Chase.

Jarod started strong. He wasn't in the pole position, but he pushed his way toward the top of the pack. It was loud, and fast, and incredibly intense. She watched one driver slam into the wall, five cars crash into one another at the second turn, and another go up in flames. Thankfully, nobody was seriously injured.

There was so much action, that first hour went by amazingly fast.

The crunching and squealing sounds coming from the

track in the next wreck had Viv cringing. She didn't know how Jarod dealt with the impact of hitting and being hit by the other cars. The anxiety of it all had her pacing on the roof.

They were getting close now. Two laps left, and Jarod was in fourth place behind Phil Reddy, Charlie Stewart, and a guy they called *Blue,* with Lachlan trailing shortly behind. That's when Lach rode up on Jarod's back end, pushing him forward. The cars started fishtailing, and she thought it was all over.

Until Jarod wrestled for control and used the push to shoot past Blue.

There was only one lap left, and Jarod was gaining on them. He pulled ahead of the other two cars inch by inch, taking the lead. And not long after, he was so far ahead that it was no question who won when they crossed the finish line.

She let out a big *whoop* and jumped up and down in celebration. Damn, she had to admit it was exciting. Scratch that. It was thrilling.

So much so that it took her a few minutes before she was able to regain her composure, which was another reason to be glad she was alone. Then she immediately went into work mode. She hit send on the press release she had ready to go, and rushed down to the inside track so she could work with Jarod's *handler* to get some good photos to include in her feature packages.

As Mel predicted, Jarod did have words with Lachlan Walker. It didn't escalate, so Viv let it go. They'd talk about that later, because once she saw him in his fire suit with that cocky grin of his, she had to fight the urge to wrap him in a hug.

She was so proud of him, but this wasn't the time to act like a pit lizard and hang all over the guy. She had work to do. In fact, she was so busy coordinating interviews and sending out material, she never had time to congratulate him. And once the sponsors arrived, all bets were off.

"You must be Vivian," Mr. Fox, the freaking head honcho of the Saturn Corp, said to her. "Good work, darlin'. Just excellent."

"Thank you, sir," she said, unable to wrap her head around the fact that she was talking to a billionaire.

"Henry told us he trusted Miranda to assign the right person, and he was right."

So Henry and Miranda do know each other.

"And I'll tell you something, if you get our boy to the Chase, I will be forever indebted to you. So keep it up now."

"I will, sir," she said, still stunned.

Mr. Fox gathered the crew, and they moved off amid a flurry of camera flashes and handshakes. Limited by the speed of her phone, she went back to her makeshift office in the bus, firing off additional photos and fielding preliminary interview questions.

Once all of her work was complete, she took the congratulatory call from her mom. From the sound of it, you would've thought Viv won the race on her own.

"You did it," her mother yelled so loudly, she had to pull the phone away from her ear.

"Pretty exciting race, wasn't it?" Viv said, unable to hide her own enthusiasm.

"I have to say, I loved every second of it. Is he there? May I congratulate him?"

"Mom," she said, insulted. "I'm not passing the phone over to him. That wouldn't be very professional. Plus, he's not here."

"Oh, honey," her mom scolded. "I'm sure he would think it was nice. I can be pretty charming, you know."

Viv had to laugh at her mother's request. Leave it to her to want to meet her client as if he was one of her college friends.

She had a nice visit with her mom, but cut it short when she saw Jarod stepping into her room. She wondered how long he had been lurking out there.

"Hey," she said, after she hung up the phone. "Are you all done?"

He nodded, finally starting to show a little wear from the race. His hair was a mess, and his eyes looked droopy. "So how's Mom?" he asked, a little more interested than she would have guessed.

There was no doubt he had been eavesdropping on her conversation again. And now he was fishing for a compliment. She may as well get it over with. "She's great, and she says congrats on the win."

Unable to hold back his grin, he said, "Your mama is watching my races now? That must mean you're talking about me again."

"Don't get a big head about it," she said, downplaying the call. "She's watching because she's interested in me and what I'm doing with you."

"Really?" He jumped on the chance to exploit any type of innuendo.

"What I'm doing with you as a *client*," she clarified.

"If that's what you have to tell yourself." He chuckled.

"But come on now, what did *you* think of the race?"

She wanted to give him some smart-ass reply, but she couldn't. Not after she witnessed what he went through during a race. "It was awesome," she said, brushing off some imaginary lint from her dress. "You were awesome."

She gritted her teeth, waiting for him to gloat. He didn't. In fact, he looked a little embarrassed.

"Thanks, Vi," he said.

"So what now?" she asked before he could say more. "Do you drink yourself silly and have someone roll you onto the chopper and deliver you home in the wee hours of the morning, or what?"

"Not this time," he said. "I have an early-morning meeting with the team, so we just pack up and head home."

"Well, that's anticlimactic," she said. "I feel like we need to *do* something."

"I have something you can do for me," he said.

"What's that?"

"Say thank you to your mom for me, and next time, pass the phone over. I don't give two licks if you think it's unprofessional."

He had *been listening.*

"Hey, speaking of unprofessional." She bypassed his comment. "What was going on with you and Lachlan Walker?"

"The idiot bump-drafted me and almost caused a spin-out." His expression instantly grew dark.

Bump-draft? She would Google that just as soon as she could.

"Do you always have problems with him during the races?" she asked. "I've heard that the two of you aren't on the best terms, and if there's something going on, I need to know about it."

"Don't worry, Vi," he said. "It's just racing business. I'm sure you have the same issues at Elite. Some people you don't quite trust. It's just smart to keep an eye on them."

Oh, she knew what he was talking about. She had one weasel of her own she needed to keep tabs on.

Chapter Twelve

She was talking to her mama about me.

That was all Jarod could think about on the drive home. He didn't know what that meant for a Yank, but it sure as heck meant something where he came from.

They had about an hour's drive left, but he didn't feel any of the relief he typically did on the way home after a race. Then again, it wasn't a typical event. The races usually invigorated him, but with all the extra interviews and publicity, he was spent. There was also the tiny issue of the woman staying in his bus over the weekend.

He was so beat, he had slept in the chopper on the way back to North Carolina. The rest helped. Though now he was completely alert and aware of that same woman sitting next to him in the passenger seat of his car.

Viv had asked if he wanted her to drive so he could sleep on the way back to his place. He had to admit, her gesture warmed him. Not that he'd ever take her up on it. He could hardly handle riding in a taxi—if there was a car in the picture, he preferred to be the person behind the wheel. Okay, he insisted on it.

To make matters worse, Viv had changed into a sundress for the trip home. She looked so fresh and innocent it was difficult to keep his eyes off her. Though he went nuts for her power suits and business clothes that commanded his attention, he loved when she was off the clock wearing her feminine dresses and casual shorts.

Even more appealing was that he knew there was another side to her prim, polished exterior—reckless and wild, untamed and unafraid. It was like he was in on a juicy secret.

God Almighty, it's going to be a long ride home.

He hadn't touched her since they supposedly *got it out of their systems* at Viv's place. Then again, she didn't come out of her room much over the weekend, and she had his schedule so jam-packed there wasn't a lot of opportunity. Probably a good thing.

Still, he couldn't keep his mind off the fact that she'd been talking about him. Nor could he ignore the way that strap on her sundress kept sliding off her shoulder.

By the time she pulled it up for the sixth time—yes, he was counting—he was more than unnerved.

At the stoplight, he damn near ripped the strap, pulling it as far up her shoulder as he could get it. "Think you can keep your clothes on while I'm trying to drive, Vi? Jesus."

She leaned into his touch until his words sank in. Then she recoiled, grabbing the light sweater that was draped over her handbag on the floor. She put it on without saying a word, and didn't say a thing the rest of the drive home.

It made him feel like shit. He wanted to apologize, but

maybe it was better this way. Everything was riding on these next few races, and he literally had a team of people counting on him. He couldn't fuck up again. Plus, he and Viv had proved that they could work together without going at it like bunnies. They just needed to keep the lines drawn and their jobs the priority.

That was the only way this would work.

• • •

When Viv arrived back in the office the following Monday, she was still feeling like an idiot. Jarod actually thought she was trying to come on to him in the car on the way back from the race. Those damn dress straps, and the way they slid off her shoulders every two seconds. *Ugh*.

That was not intentional.

She couldn't deny that she wore the dress for him—she upped her game whenever he was around. But she didn't mean to be falling out of the thing. What was worse? He seemed repulsed by it.

Replaying the scene—and Jarod's words—over and over again put her in quite a state. By the time she got to Elite, she was officially a hot mess.

Though Miranda had authorized her time away from the office during this project, Viv needed to put some space between her and Jarod. She had three days before they left for Florida, and she just couldn't be holed up with him in his house for that long. So she planned to work in the office at the beginning of the week and join him on Wednesday.

Once she found out Miranda would be away on business, she called Mel to tell her she was coming in. Miranda was gone almost 50 percent of the time, which was the only reason Viv had lasted at Elite as long as she had.

When she walked into her office, it looked like a party. Mel had the room decked out with checkered balloons and enlarged copies of all the media coverage she helped secure after Jarod's win.

Yep, she had made the right decision coming in to work.

"Vivi," Mel said, as she barged in with Soph, Jess, and a few other members of the team. "Congratulations on all the metro sports coverage. This is huge."

It was a big win for her, and more importantly for Jarod. There were features and roundup stories in more than fifty newspapers across the country. It was an amazing start. Still, Viv had her eyes on bigger things for the campaign, and if Jarod didn't fire her, she knew she'd get there.

"You guys are the best," she said, taking the cupcake that Jess offered. "But you didn't have to do this."

"You sounded down on the phone," Mel said. "We just wanted to give you a little pick-me-up and celebrate. Look at all this excellent coverage"—Mel flicked her wrist at the articles plastered on the walls—"in just one weekend."

Mel always knew exactly how to make her feel better. She wished she could take her on the road for moral support. Not possible, but a nice thought.

They celebrated for a few minutes, and Viv devoured the cupcake, but it was short-lived.

"Viv, let's chat," Miranda said as she walked by the office, not stopping to join in the festivities. For anyone who didn't know the Ice Queen, it would've sounded like a sweet request. But Viv knew better, she'd been summoned.

Shit, shit, shit. Why is she here?

Miranda was marked out for the entire day, she was sure of it.

Mel cringed once Miranda was out of sight. "She was supposed to be in Nashville all day, I swear."

They all stood frozen for a moment, when Fredrick stuck his weaselly nose inside.

"Not expecting Miranda today, ladies?" he said. "Strange, that dang log always seems to be wrong lately."

"It's okay," Viv blew him off. She would not let him get to her. "I had to check in with her sooner or later anyway." She took a breath and headed out the door, leaving the others scrambling to remove all signs of the celebration.

"You wanted to see me," Viv said after knocking twice on Miranda's door. The Ice Queen had them all trained in this particular fashion. No more than two knocks.

"Come in," Miranda said. "And tell me why you are here instead of taking care of your client?"

"I am taking care of him," she said. "I'm planning his meet-and-greet for the race in Florida this weekend."

"Yes, but I thought we agreed that you would work from the Cage estate so he wouldn't have to come to Atlanta for counsel."

"He's fine," she said. "Actually, I think he needs some space."

"Not according to his manager," Miranda snapped, and Viv wondered why she was keeping her relationship with Henry a secret. If the sponsors knew about it, it couldn't be all that juicy.

But right now, Viv was in no place to ask.

"What's going on?"

"He told me that Jarod was out of sorts after the last

race," Miranda said. "And I don't have to tell you, we need his head in the game if he's going to make it to the Chase."

"I'm not sure what I can do about his emotional state, Miranda." Viv knew that wasn't the tone to take with her boss, but she was out of sorts herself.

"This is part of your job." Miranda splayed her hands on her desk. "Keeping him comfortable and confident."

"I'm not sure I know how to do that."

"Of course you don't." Miranda stood up. "You've been here almost two years and you still haven't acclimated to the culture at all. It's not always about business, Viv. Try connecting with him. Try being a friend. How do you think I made all my connections through the years? By being the Ice Queen?"

Viv's mouth dropped open.

"Oh, don't look so surprised," she said. "I know what y'all say about me. But there has to be more to me than that, don't you think? To consistently have the level of business we have at Elite? I take it all very personally. And when I choose to work with someone, I'm all in. This is what I haven't seen from you yet. Yes, you do the right things. Your campaigns are flawless, but where is the passion?"

"I have passion," Viv said, fully aware that she sounded like a child, once again. Miranda brought it out in her. "I do."

"Then get out there and prove it," Miranda said.

She was dismissed.

Chapter Thirteen

When Vi's car pulled up the day before they were supposed to leave for the next race, he worried that she was there to break up with him—professionally speaking. He couldn't blame her. He'd been hot and cold with her since they met. A downright ass at times. And she wasn't the only person who had to deal with his wrath. He'd chewed out Henry and a few other guys on the crew before he could get his wits about him.

Though he knew Miranda had arranged for Vi to stay at his place between races, she'd made some excuse to go home after Indy. And that was the last thing he heard from her in two days.

He walked out to the drive, slow and steady, already working on his speech to convince her to stay. As difficult as it was to be around her with all the sexual tension threatening to strangle him on a daily basis, it was even worse without her.

She calmed him as much as she revved him up. But hell, he was a grown-ass man who should be able to handle a relationship with a woman that didn't end with them doing the horizontal dance between the sheets. He'd tell her as much if he had to.

Point was, he wasn't going to lose her.

"I have good news," she said, jumping out of that ridiculous clown car with a heart-stopping smile spread across her face. Leave it to her Northern sensibilities to jump right to the point, without so much as stopping to say hello.

Funny, that no longer bothered him. Maybe there was something to her way of doing things. No pretense, always moving forward—onward and upward. Right now that sounded pretty good to him.

Plus, she wasn't pissed, and that was always a welcome sign.

"What do ya got for me, Yank?" he said, taking her bag when she dragged it from the car.

The bag was another welcome sign, and he found he could breathe a little easier.

"Your meet-and-greet in Florida is standing room only," she said, proudly. "And I got you a feature in the *Daytona Beach News-Journal*."

"Features are good, right?" he asked, keeping his eyes on her face. Oh yeah, he noticed those little shorts on her impossibly long legs—it made no damn sense that they could be so long when she barely reached his chest with heels on—but he wouldn't let them distract him.

"No," she said. "Features are fucking fantastic. They allow us to show another side of you—the likable side."

Don't say fuck, Vi.

He quickly readjusted himself before she could see what her cursing did to him.

"Didn't know you thought I had a likable side," he said.

"I may have seen it once or twice," she joked.

"I've been a real ornery bastard with you, and I'm sorry about that."

"And I've been a coldhearted Yank to you." She put out her hand. "How about we call a truce?"

He took her hand, feeling the same sparks he did the first time. "I can live with that."

"So we're good?" she asked. "Because we have a lot of work to do."

"We're better than good, Vi," he said.

But how long could he keep it that way?

• • •

Jarod had looked shocked when she came rolling up to his house. Mr. B was on his riding lawn mower at the gate and waved her in. She had no idea whether she'd be welcomed or turned away.

She knew she should've made small talk once he met her in the driveway, asked how he'd been over the past two days. Maybe address what had happened in the car on the way home from the race. She'd tried, but when her hands went clammy and her stomach turned, she just started to blabber about work. She didn't know any other way.

He didn't seem to mind, and after the shock wore off, he almost looked happy to see her. At least she hoped so.

They needed to get back into a routine to cut through the awkwardness. So Viv went right to work. She was mostly business during the day, though she used a little softer touch when she prepared Jarod for the interview.

Try being a friend to him.

Miranda's unexpected words stuck with her. So that's what she tried to do. She put herself in Jarod's position and helped him work through his answers to the questions she expected the reporter to ask. This time, instead of badgering him when he started to shut down, she gave him options to bridge to another topic—answering the question without really answering. It was a key technique used in politics. She armed him with information, tools, and choices.

It seemed to work.

Jarod wasn't nervous when she introduced him to the reporter over the phone. His face didn't sour like it usually did, and she said a silent prayer.

"So, Mr. Cage," the reporter said. "What do you like about our little speedway in Daytona?"

"It's always been one of my favorites," Jarod answered, winking at Viv. "Everything about it is state-of-the-art."

Jarod was charming and fun, and so far the reporter was respectful. But after the easy questions, she held her breath, knowing what was coming next.

"So, Mr. Cage, we're not going to see a repeat of your offtrack behavior this weekend, like what you did in Charlotte, are we?"

Boom.

Viv nodded, her way of telling him to go on. She gently placed her hand over his.

"Well, there will be none of that going on in Daytona," Jarod answered. "I'm here for a *repeat* of what I did at the 500 in February, and to meet some of the best racing fans in the world. Daytona is special that way."

Jarod went on to share some of his favorite races and experiences, and Viv found herself immersed in his stories. She almost forgot she was supposed to be working.

"Daytona has seen some of the best racing has to offer," he said.

"It really has, hasn't it?" the reporter said, seeming to get sidetracked. "I see you're also hosting the Kids of Valor during the race."

Bingo.

Now Jarod had the chance to talk about his work with the kids, and about his father's work in the army before he started racing, which was really fascinating because Jarod never discussed him. It was incredibly moving to listen to him talk about his dad, and the way Henry stepped in to help the family while his father was away.

So much about her bad-boy race car driver was beginning to make sense.

"You did great," she told him when the phone interview was finished.

"Sure I didn't bore that man to tears?" he asked.

"Are you kidding?" she said. "You had him eating out of the palm of your hand, and you bridged from his tough question perfectly. It wasn't stiff or contrived, because you gave him something real."

"I'm not going to lie." He ran his hand through his thick mop, and she did her yoga breathing to help fight through the urge to put her own hand all up in that sexy hair. "I still didn't care for telling him my personal shit, but it was easier with you here."

"I'm glad," she said, feeling her insides go all toasty.

"You should be proud of the work you do with those kids, you know. It's a big deal giving your time like that."

"No," he said. "It's a big deal what I get back from them. I get more than I give, trust me on that."

"My yogi always says, 'The best way to find yourself is to lose yourself in the service of others.'"

"Yogi." He shook his head. "Vi, I like you, I really do, but you're a little out there sometimes."

She laughed, appreciating the way he lightened the mood.

"Don't knock it until you try it," she said before fully realizing what she was saying. Now there was an excellent idea: get Jarod into yoga. Oh, she'd absolutely work on making that happen.

"Yeah, yeah." He stood up. "I'm just glad it's done. I'm also starving. Let's go to the kitchen to see if Mrs. B. has our shrimp and grits ready yet."

"I let her off early," she said.

"*What?*" She could tell he was trying not to raise his voice. "Why? It's the night before a race weekend. I need my shrimp and grits, Vi."

"Oh don't be such a stick-in-the-mud," she said. "I'm fixing to make you something really special."

"Girl, I know you didn't make fun of my accent."

"Nah." She giggled. "You must be wearing off on me. Now come on. I'm going to introduce you to comfort food… Yankee style."

Jarod sucked in a breath, clearly not trusting her, but when they went into the kitchen it smelled like heaven.

She'd put the dish together before the interview, while Jarod was on a call with his crew. Viv arranged everything from Atlanta, determined to show Jarod that she also had a likable side. Mrs. B did the grocery shopping for her last night.

He started digging in even before she was able to put it on plates.

"I can't believe you eat this stuff up there," he said. "I thought all you ate was grilled chicken and salad. Rabbit food."

"I personally don't eat this kind of thing often," she said. "But lobster rolls are the ultimate comfort food."

Viv nudged Jarod out of the way so she could plate up their meals and get them to the table.

They ate until they were ready to burst, and then plopped in front of the TV on Jarod's overstuffed sofa. It wasn't sleek and modern like the furniture at her place, but it sure was comfortable.

"Can I see the remote?" she asked, noticing the time.

"It's a clicker," he said, pointing it at her. "And no, you may not."

"That's rude." She tried to pry it from his hand.

"House rules," he said. "Sorry, babe."

She continued to make a play for it, but this time he moved too fast. And she went falling right on top of him.

He was warm, and ohmygod, hard as a rock. They stayed there, unmoving, for a second, or maybe twenty. He looked at her, his lids hooded and his pupils black. Her brain sounded off an alarm: danger, danger, danger.

She scrambled off him and he flew to the other side of the couch.

And after they both caught their breath, he threw the remote control to her. "Here, I guess you can choose."

• • •

Just get through the night, Cage. And whatever you do, don't look at her legs.

Viv found *The West Wing* on some cable channel, but he didn't hear a word of it. His brain had short-circuited when her tiny and very responsive body came crashing down on top of him.

And when they each went into their separate rooms after the show was over, he had a hard time forming the words "good night."

By the time they got to Daytona, he found his willpower was stronger. Maybe the longer he was with her, the more immune he'd become.

Or not.

From his perch inside his bus, he was treated to the most spectacular wake-up call. She started every day this way—out front contorting that tight body into positions even he hadn't seen. His mind went to dirty places watching her move.

"I see you there in the window, Cage," Vi said, as she was bent over in some yoga position on her mat outside the bus. "Get out here and join me. And bring a towel."

He did as she said, laying a bath towel next to Viv's mat.

Why the fuck not? Yoga was supposed to help with relaxation, right?

"This is downward facing dog," she said with her ass high in the air.

Okay, so this was either the best idea he'd ever had, or the worst.

"I recognize this one," he said with a grin, and just to make things even, he took off his shirt. If she was going to tempt him in this way, he'd try his damnedest to do the same.

Her deep inhale was all he needed to hear. He lowered his head and hands, trying to match her movements.

"Good," she said, her cheeks stained pink. "Get used to this position, because we always come back here. I'm in the middle of a sun salutation, so just follow along. From here, we move into plank—like a push-up."

She looked over at him and cleared her throat. "Yep, you have that one down perfectly. Then bend your arms and hold for a breath, before arching up into cobra."

Shit, the moves kept getting better.

They moved through mountain pose, some kind of fold, a lunge, and ended with their hands folded in prayer. At the end of it, he wasn't more relaxed.

He also wasn't a quitter, so he joined her the following morning, and the next. Until he found himself holding a third-place trophy on Sunday.

New Hampshire went much the same way. They'd start with yoga, do their separate things during the day, and end in the evening, fighting over the clicker. It was a happy arrangement.

If only they could bring those yoga moves to the bedroom…then he'd call their situation close to perfect.

Chapter Fourteen

When they hit Bristol, Viv finally felt like she had mastered the sport. Her studying and observations, the routine surrounding race days, it had taken some time to grasp, but she now knew Jarod's schedule down to the minute.

If only she could get a handle on Kelsey. As usual, she was the first to stop in at each race. Always dressed to the nines, she greeted Jarod with a hug. It was the worst part of the weekend.

She'd usually take him away for an hour and then deliver him back to the bus, like he wasn't capable of walking back on his own. Viv checked her watch and, yup, a glance out the motor home window showed Miss Personality ferrying Jarod back on her little pink golf cart. Bleh.

Viv pretended not to hover, like she hadn't been counting down the minutes to his return, but she was already on her feet with the door open.

"Be sure to pick a good one now," Kelsey called out as

she drove off. "You know how the crowd loves a show."

Jarod slipped past her to enter the motor coach. "A good what?" Viv asked once they were alone. She was not going to be shut out.

"A song," Jarod answered, leaning up against the table in the kitchen, keeping his distance.

"For what?"

"It's a tradition at Bristol. When the guys—and actually two gals for this race—are introduced before qualifying, they play a song, and the drivers address the fans. It's all for show, and as you might have guessed, I fucking hate it."

"Are you crazy?" She grabbed her phone and started searching for songs. "This is exactly the kind of stuff you need to let me handle. No opportunity for publicity is too small. You've got to tell me about this stuff."

"That's hard for me to do." Jarod took an apple from the fruit bowl Viv put on the table and sank his teeth into it with a loud bite. "I don't care about that shit. I don't even think about it."

"You need to care. Everything you do at this point makes a difference. It's a great angle. Bad boy does good. Damn, Jarod, we could've gotten one of your Little Brothers from your volunteer work to do it with you."

"I will not exploit the few good things I do to better my image." He bristled. "I won't use the kids that way."

She crossed her arms. "The kids would love it, you idiot. It's a win-win."

"No," he said, never looking up from his stupid piece of fruit.

"No?" Viv moved closer to him, not at all understanding why he was making such a big deal out of this.

"You heard me," he said on her approach. "I'm not doing it."

"Fine." She snagged his apple and took a bite. "But I will be working on your song and your speech."

"I won't grovel, Vi. And also, don't make me look like an ass-lick in front of my peers."

"You need to trust me on this." She gave him a playful punch him in the shoulder, and he snaked an arm around her, locking her flailing limb in place. "Can you do that, *baby*?" She ignored the submissive positions he put her in, knowing she could get her way with words.

It had been too long since they played this game. Oh, the tension had been simmering between them, there was no doubt of that. And their morning yoga sessions had become an exercise in self-control. Hell, she'd been dumb with lust pretty much 24-7. It was amazing she was able to do her job. But they'd had an unspoken no-touching rule. Her light shoulder punch had kicked that gate wide open. Thank God.

"Damn it, woman." He squeezed tighter. "Don't use the baby on me or you're going to get it."

"Can't handle my sweet talk?" She shimmied against him, making no move to leave his arms.

"Let me take you into the back of the bus and show you."

Tempting. Oh so tempting. But she had to play it cool. "You mean one of the bedrooms in this million-dollar motor coach you live in?"

"*We* live in," he said in the shell of her ear.

PR Rule Number 22: Do not stray from the plan.

"You go on now," she told him. "I have work to do before tonight."

• • •

The track was a madhouse that night. Fans and reporters gathered in the stands on the infield, surrounding what Viv would describe as a red carpet catwalk. Jarod probably had some macho word for it, but it honestly looked like a catwalk and there was literally a red carpet rolled down the center. Viv handed over the music to the event coordinators as all the drivers gathered behind a screen ready to make their entrance.

Jarod was wearing a black fire suit, and it was quickly becoming Viv's favorite male attire—especially on her client. She couldn't get enough of him in it. In fact, she hadn't been able to think of much else all day.

And that explained what happened next.

Earlier, Viv was entertaining herself, making up funny speeches and music for Jarod. He was out for a long time, and she had finished everything they needed. The motor coach was quiet, and she needed to do something so she wouldn't die of boredom. She pulled up the most annoying songs she could come up with. "Pour Some Sugar on Me" and "I Touch Myself" worked particularly well.

After playing around for a few hours, she decided to go with Johnny Cash's "I Walk the Line." A classic. It played to the fanbase, showed respect, and who didn't love a man down and out trying to do right? It was perfect. His introduction? Even better.

"I'm Jarod Cage in the number nine Toyota. I thank God to be here tonight with y'all."

He was going right after the female driver Cassie Fine,

who was a little wild. The contrast was perfect.

But it didn't go down like that. Not even close.

There was no Johnny Cash. Instead, Jarod walked down the runway to "I Touch Myself," the lovely ditty about a woman masturbating.

Laughter erupted, followed by some boos. It looked like it was Jarod's words to the female driver ahead of him. It seemed incredibly disrespectful, and as Jarod would say, made him look like a complete ass-lick.

He was so frazzled when he got up to the microphone, the introduction went something like, "Thank God, I'm Jarod Cage y'all."

It was bad.

And then he had to go off and try to get his highest speed to qualify for Sunday's race in just two laps.

He managed to do that. Just barely.

Chapter Fifteen

"What in the actual fuck?" Jarod shouted when he got back to the bus.

"Shit, I'm so sorry." Viv came out of her room to find him pacing up and down the length of the bus. "It's my fault. Totally my fault. I gave them the wrong music. I wasn't thinking. It's just you've been strutting around in that fucking fire suit all day."

Huh? He stopped midstride. "What does that have to do with anything?"

"I can't think straight when I see you in that thing," she blurted. The back wall of the motor coach was holding her up. "I just can't do this. We're so close in the bus, but then we go to bed each night in our own rooms, and I *didn't* get it out of my system. Okay? I'm messing up, saying the wrong thing all the time. I'm a freaking liability for you at this point."

That's when Jarod truly lost it. His body started to shake, his eyes glassy, his mouth…turned up in a grin as he released the loudest belly laugh. He knew exactly what her babbling outburst was all about. Hell, he'd been living with the worst case of blue balls known to man. But he'd thought that's what she wanted.

Fuck that, it's what he wanted, because what they had was too unstable. He couldn't trust it, and he didn't want to be imprisoned by it. So he lied to himself and to Vi.

But they were going to have to do something about it before they screwed up both of their careers. Though he had to appreciate the humor of the situation. He couldn't stop laughing, and soon Vi was giggling along with him. The relief was like a balm to the soul.

"Jesus, did you hear what I said up there?" he asked.

"Thank God, I'm Jarod Cage y'all," she said between fits of laughter.

"I sounded like a total ass. But I guess it was the ultimate compliment to Cassie."

"Was she pissed?" Viv cringed.

"Hell, no. She loved every second of it."

"So you're not upset." She bit her lip.

"No, hon. I'm not. It surprised me, obviously from my intro. But it was actually friggin' hilarious." He sank onto the couch, relief and something pretty close to joy, yes, friggin' *joy*, making his bones feel all lax and his shoulders lighter.

"But you almost didn't quality," she said, completely changing her demeanor. "I thought you were upset."

"Nah, I was just having a little problem with the car," he said, feeling terrible that she was back here thinking his performance was due to her. "Henry's on it now. We should be fine come race time."

She expelled a deep breath. "Okay, so now we just need

to do some damage control."

"Already did," he said, proudly.

"What? How?"

"After I was done taking my turns, I chatted with some reporters. I told them that the guys were messing with me. They got a good laugh. Then I launched into my real song, and how I am trying to walk the line and do better and be better. I want to be able to talk to my fans—especially the kids—with pride."

Her mouth hung open. "You went to them?"

"Yep."

"How'd they react?"

He shrugged. "Surprised, I guess. But once I opened up, it was better."

"See," she squealed. "See. They just need to see the real you. I'm so happy. So proud of you. I know it wasn't easy. But that was the right thing. Exactly the right thing."

"I guess that means you aren't a liability. I think I should keep you around."

"I was so worried. You have no idea. I feel like a thousand-pound weight is off my shoulders."

"So about your obsession with my fire suit. We can't have you making mistakes because you're thinking with your—"

"Don't say it." She cuffed his shoulder. "God, you are so crude."

"And you love it. Which reminds me, all day I've been wondering if you're wearing panties. I can't see a trace of a line in these little pants—not even the outline of a thong—I've looked. It's driving me insane. That's why I had trouble, actually. You've got me wound so tight."

She didn't tell him what he was desperate to know. She

didn't say a word.

Fire sparked in her eyes as she went to him. Rising on her tiptoes, she brushed her lips on the underside of his jaw. Slow at first. But her little mouth grew greedy, taking what she wanted. She dived into his neck with hot, wet kisses.

Then she peeled away, just long enough to whip off her shirt, before she went right for the piece of him that had been neglected most of all. With a sure hand, she cupped him over his fire suit.

"Fuck, yes," Jarod said as he picked her up and carried her to the back room of the motor home. "My thoughts exactly."

"It's just to relieve our stress so we can do our jobs," she told him as her legs locked around his hips.

"Strictly business," he agreed.

Jarod kicked the door shut and had Viv half undressed and on the bed in record time. The hum of engines and fans muffled in the background. It made for the sexiest soundtrack for what Jarod did next.

He propped her on the edge of the bed and knelt down before her. Slowing removing the pants that had him aching for her.

Christ, she didn't have panties on.

"Didn't this seam rub you all day?" he asked, his voice so strained that the words hurt coming out.

Viv nodded.

She'd done this on purpose. Not to torture him, but herself. Holy shit, that was hot.

"Vi Blake, you are insatiable."

"You make me this way." She ran a hand through his hair and pulled.

Damn, she had no idea what she did to him. Especially after today's stunt. It wouldn't be long before she'd find out.

"I have never been like this," she whimpered. "Never been off my game."

"Oh baby, I'd say you were right on your game." He spread her legs for him. "So on."

He'd been with enthusiastic women before, but with Vi it was different. The situation was never contrived, and she wasn't posed or fake. He'd never been so in sync with someone physically.

She was glistening with arousal. The sight brought out an animalistic need in him so great, he had to bite back a growl. He wanted to consume and be consumed. With no idea how long he'd have this full-access pass to Vi in this way, he prepared to savor each and every second.

He moved his fingers to her opening, but something stopped him. This was not how he wanted to take her. And this wasn't the part of him he wanted inside her.

Crawling up her body, he pushed her into the mattress, sheathed himself with a condom, and waited.

Her eyes continued to burn, but this time—for reasons he couldn't name—he wanted them in focus as they became one.

When she finally met his gaze, he rewarded her by forcing the tip of his erection into her. And he stopped once again.

Vi's mouth opened…and he vowed to claim that next.

Her muscles contracted around the head of his cock, and he was lost in a wave of lust. This wasn't going to be what he wanted, he knew that now. His desire was fierce, and his blood boiled under his skin. Rather than slow and savoring, it was going to be fast and rough.

As he was processing, trying to get a hold of his emotions—as much as his physical state—he let instinct take over and plunged into her with such raw force, they both cried out.

He pulled out slowly, only to do it again. But this time, she shifted her body weight so fast, she was on top of him the very next moment, satisfying her own desire. He let her take what she wanted as she straddled his waist.

She moaned, tossing her hair back, rapture playing across her fucking beautiful face. Damn, *he* did this to her. It was better than any high he'd ever felt crossing a finish line. Yet he hadn't finished with her. Not by any stretch of the imagination.

She rode him slow and steady. He groaned, in both pain and ecstasy, as his balls pulled tight. His little Vi was under the illusion *she* was in control. Sure, he'd let her think so.

For a few short minutes.

Then he latched his hands around her tiny waist, easing her off his throbbing length, before slamming back inside. Once, twice, three times. He watched the illusion shatter into unrecognizable shards of control.

"Jarod," she gritted, digging her fingernails into his chest.

Yep, he was back in the driver's seat. As he liked it.

It was a battle for control in the dirtiest kind of race. And they wouldn't know who won until they reached the end. But as the pressure inside him reached an unbearable level, he had only one option.

Let her win.

She drove them like a pro, swift and thorough, bringing them so close to the finish line. But never all the way. Her hips slamming against his, locking. Vi brought them to the brink of bliss and them pulled back. She rode them straight along the edge.

Slow. Fast. Slow. Faster.

The coiling of pleasure inside him threatened to unravel. He'd need to push her over that edge…soon.

In a moment of clarity, he reached a hand between them to touch her where she needed it most. With his thumb, he pushed on that oversensitive bundle of nerves, and she almost shot off the bed. Her legs trembled, and she was having trouble staying upright. He tightened his hold on her hip, keeping her in place.

"I've got you, Vi." He worked her clit again in quick little circles. "You can let go."

That was all it took. Vi stilled for a few seconds before her muscles gripped him like a vise, contracting around his throbbing cock as she shattered.

Her head lobbed back on her neck, and a string of incoherent pleas spilled from her lips as she continued to ride it out. Jarod's own pressure mounted, begging for release. The last of the spasms ripped through her—that's what did him in and pushed him over the edge.

With one last thrust of his hips, he was overcome with pleasure, sated in a way that nearly wrecked him. He couldn't move for a long time after that.

Maybe there was something to riding shotgun every now and then.

• • •

Bristol brought another third-place win for Jarod, and several more orgasms for the both of them. "Just one more time" became their mantra—their only way of surviving their living arrangement.

Sadly, it didn't solve everything.

Every race brought them one step closer to the Chase. Jarod did his best to keep his anxiety in check, but damn near everybody at the track, on his crew, and among his sponsors was amped up. Vi sensed it, too. She sat beside him on a plastic chair outside their bus, her foot tap-tap-tapping. He normally appreciated her high-energy, plow-forward approach, but sensing her nervousness was only compounding his own. Oh, he had a couple of ideas for how they could burn off some of that tension, but with so many people underfoot, they couldn't sneak inside without it being totally obvious. Damn it.

He raked a hand through his hair.

Vi shot to her feet. "Let's get out of here for a while," she said. "You're on edge, and I'm feeling a bit like a goldfish in a fishbowl."

Yeah. It seemed like all eyes on the field somehow gravitated toward their motor coach.

"And I'm hungry," she went on. "A burger and a beer might do us some good."

"Miss Discipline wants to fuck up my schedule the night before the qualifier, are you for real?" She held out her hand, and he allowed her to tug him to his feet.

"Okay, how about salad and water?" she suggested. "Though I think I might need a beer. All this testosterone around here is making me stabby."

"Fine," he said. "Let's go."

"Wait. I'd like to clean up a little," she said.

"The only kind of bar we're going to find around here is a honky-tonk. So trust me, you're overdressed. Come on."

Jarod led her through the motor coach village to his garage, where he had a street car waiting for him. The two jumped into an inconspicuous Toyota sedan, and he drove around town until they found a suitable option. He'd had a couple of places in mind, but he gauged how busy they were. He loved his fans, but he didn't want to be bum-rushed or forced to be "on." That was exactly the kind of thing that had him so keyed up in the first place.

He recalled a local hangout, a spot he'd been to a few years back, and he had Vi queue it up on her phone's GPS. As he pulled into the gravel-strewn parking lot, he saw that the place hadn't changed a bit. The red painted sign proclaiming the name of the bar still hung at a precarious angle, making him think that sometime soon an unlucky patron would become victim to its inevitable fall. Assorted neon signs in the blacked-out windows showcased about ninety kinds of beer. It was lowbrow—and just as he liked it. He guided Vi through the door and paused.

They'd renovated the inside, opening it up to an outdoor oasis. The formerly sawdust-covered floor now appeared to be covered in sand. Compliments of the open back deck with its tiki theme and broad expanse of volleyball nets, cornhole stations, and fire pits.

Turned out it was more beach bar than honky-tonk. Nice. Jarod noted the sandpit to the left with an assortment of tables and a long area for playing horseshoes. He felt his competitive streak rear its ugly head.

Once they found a seat, he went to the bar and picked up a soda water for himself and a Corona for Vi. He returned and lounged in the chair beside her.

"I put in our burger orders," he said.

She shoved the lime in her beer and quirked a brow. "What happened to your salad?"

"I have that coming, too, with my bison burger."

Viv crinkled her nose.

"Great protein, and much leaner and healthier. I will be well on my way for tomorrow."

"I have no doubt." She tilted her head back and took a long sip, the smooth column of her neck flexing as she swallowed. Maybe they should've stayed back at the bus.

"You're a sure bet," she told him, and damn if that wasn't a boost to his ego. "I've been watching." She set her beer on the table and inclined her head toward the sandy tract. "Come on. Let me kick your ass in horseshoes."

He laughed and found himself feeling pretty damn good, the stress and tension of the track—of the Chase—momentarily forgotten. Once again, he had to acknowledge that Vi was right. Getting out of the crazy and into a relaxed game with his feet in the sand was just what the doctor ordered. She played to win, angling and concentrating with each toss, and Jarod didn't even bat an eye. Actually, he gave her a series of high fives and picked her up and spun her around when she got three ringers in a row.

He wasn't focused on winning so much as he was focused on *her*. And it made for one hell of an enjoyable night.

Until Phil showed up.

Chapter Sixteen

Viv hated the guy. His nickname was enough to make her gag. *Phil Reddy Wip.* Seriously? She tried to angle herself to block Jarod's view. Rather than distract him, it seemed to draw his attention.

"Fuck me," Jarod said when he spotted him.

His whole body tensed, shoulders squaring, hands flexing into fists at his side. Viv was worried as he switched gears in a matter of seconds. Honestly, it scared her a little.

Phil was your stereotypical driver. Good ol' boy with a cowboy hat, boots, and a big…belt buckle. He was a loser who happened to believe he was God's gift to the vagina. She'd caught glimpses of him in his gaudy golf cart as he ferried several pit lizards to and from his motor coach at every race.

She had never been more repulsed by a man.

He had not one but three gals from the track tangled around him right now, and all Viv could wonder was if you could catch an STD from casual contact.

"Well, look at that, girls," Phil announced. "It's my good buddy, J.C. And his little woman. Let's go say hello."

He yanked off his cowboy boots and socks and tossed them to the side, moaning when his feet hit the sand. The girls trailed right behind him.

Viv thought she might be sick.

Jarod took a step forward. "She's my PR director, dumbass."

"Whatever you say, brother." Phil punched him in the shoulder. "I'm just looking forward to the video play-by-play after you take her home." He cackled.

Jarod was in his face before the asshole finished his sentence. Hands grabbing Phil's shirt. The pit lizards' eyes lit up with excitement. Jesus.

So much for a relaxing night out.

Part of Viv loved Jarod's protective streak. The other part wondered why he was stupid enough to fall into Phil's trap.

He lifted Phil's feet off the ground. "Say shit like that again and you'll be sucking your protein bars through a straw."

"Whoa, friend." Phil patted Jarod's arms and laughed.

Oh no he didn't.

Jarod stiffened like a road-raged commuter in East Coast traffic. She prepared herself for the worst.

"I'm just playing," Phil said, sleazy grin in place. "We thought maybe y'all would be interested in a friendly game of horseshoes."

And wouldn't you know, Jarod couldn't turn away from a challenge.

Idiot.

Viv and Phil took their places at one end of the pit and Jarod stood next to the redhead at the opposite end, while the two other lizards sat and watched from the patio.

It was ridiculous, but her palms went clammy as she held the horseshoes in her hands. She wouldn't deny that she also had a competitive side, but mostly she wanted to get rid of these freaks so she could go back to her evening with Jarod.

PR Rule Number 20: Sometimes you need to take one for the team.

She planted her feet in the sand and let the first shoe fly. The metal *clank* was music to her ears as she wrapped it around the post. Phil shifted his feet.

Clank.

The second shoe smacked the post before dropping right on top of the first. She tried not to smirk.

Take that, bitches.

The redhead wasn't as lucky. Neither was Phil.

Viv and Jarod took the lead immediately. She knew her opponent underestimated her mad horseshoe skills, and that pleased her quite a bit.

Jarod winked at her and she smiled like a lovesick schoolgirl. They so had this.

Phil blathered on the entire game. Viv wasn't even sure what he was saying, since she opted to tune him out. She wasn't going to let him ruin their night. Once they won the game, they were so outta there.

The next shot she took made that glorious *clank*ing sound once again. It wrapped around the post, pirouetting in two lovely circles.

"Hot damn," Phil said. "This girl is smokin'."

Now, typically, something like that would've been all it would take to set Jarod off. He was possessive and hotheaded, not to mention he clearly despised Phil. But it was what the fool did next that had Jarod lunging across the sand pit at Phil's throat.

It was like it happened in slow motion.

Viv released the horseshoe. It spun around the post.

Jarod pumped an arm in celebration, and she jumped into an embarrassing move from her cheerleading days.

And then, Reddy Wip was all over her ass. Like literally.

Oh yeah, he joined the celebration by grabbing a huge handful of booty.

Viv didn't even have time to slap him, because Jarod flew through the air like a flipping Bengal tiger and dropped ol' Reddy Wip to the ground.

It was a bar fight of epic proportions. Even the best spin doctor in the world couldn't contain what transpired in the next minute.

"Jarod," she screamed, trying to wedge her way in the middle of them. Not really a smart move on her behalf, with them grappling and fists flying.

"Get out of here, Viv," Jarod growled. "Now."

A crowd began to gather, but when Viv tried to contain it, Pit Lizard Number One came gunning for her.

Oh, hell no, she wasn't going to get wrapped up in this. Miranda would shit a brick and send her packing if she was involved in a bar brawl. There was no way she was going to put up her dukes.

Pit Lizards Two and Three moved down to the sand, cheering on the redhead, who took out her earrings, preparing for a fight. She stalked closer. Shit.

Viv may have peed her pants a little. She hadn't seen a skank prepare to throw down since circa 2009 at an Alpha Chi Omega social. And it was nothing like this. The redhead knew what she was doing.

As Red descended, Viv clenched her fist, trying to remember if the thumb went on the inside or outside when punching. So much for sitting this one out.

Jarod looked over at the perfect time. He had Phil right where he wanted him and was a good half dozen punches in when he caught Pit Lizard One headed toward Viv. He called out to warn her, which was really more of a distraction than a warning, and on instinct, Viv skillfully ducked and stuck out a leg. The redhead went boobs-first into the sand.

That's when the cameras whipped out, and when Viv hightailed it to safety. Then she got on the phone with the owners of the team. She knew she'd locked them in on speed-dial for a reason.

She'd made good with them from the very start of the campaign. A point she hoped would save their asses now.

PR Rule Number 7: Build goodwill with everyone you can. Never know when you'll need them.

Her call was answered on the second ring.

She kept an eye on Jarod. He immediately calmed once the bouncers arrived to break up the tussle. The patrons from the volleyball pits and inside the bar eventually went back to their beers and conversations, leaving her to focus on charming the big dogs. And, thanks to the Ice Queen's extensive training, she was good on the fly. Good thing—because it would take all her expertise to spin this pretty.

The first minute of her explanation to Chip Scott—*the* flippin' Chip Scott, was met with stony silence. But the owners now looked at her as a second daughter, so when she told them Jarod was defending her honor, it actually scored him a few points. Mr. Scott even promised to talk to the sponsors.

The result of her quick thinking couldn't have been more than apparent once they arrived back at the bus that night. The story was in the top news block on ESPN, complete with the gawker's video.

Jarod was unusually quiet as they listened in. He hadn't said a word on the way home, either. Viv nestled next to him while they sat on the sofa watching the latest damage to his reputation become public fodder. This time, it was all on her. But Jarod didn't push her away, so at least that was a good sign.

"That's right, folks," the sportscaster said. "Jarod Cage and Phil Reddy went at it in a good old-fashioned bar fight. Though neither driver would confirm exactly what started the altercation.

"Chip Scott, the owner of Cage's racing team, said in a statement that the video captured by patrons at the bar didn't show what caused the altercation, and after hearing the story from a reliable source, he confirmed Cage was not in the wrong."

Thank God her call worked.

"You talked to the owners already?" Jarod asked, not looking away from the TV.

"Yeah, from the sidelines at the bar," she admitted. He'd been too busy glaring at Wip Shit to notice. "Surprisingly, you may have won a few points with those old coots after tonight."

"I didn't do it to win any points," he said before reaching for the remote control and changing the channel.

"I know, and I'm sorry," she said. "This one was all on me."

"Stop it," he said, tucking a rogue curl that escaped

during her almost-brawl behind her ear. "But Vi, may I ask what you were going to do if Big Red got a hold of you?"

"I have no idea. This was so not in job description, and I am not designed for fighting."

"No shit." Jarod grinned.

"I didn't think it was possible," she said, making her way into the kitchen. "But I'm wondering now if we are more trouble together."

"We're something together, that's for sure."

"So what about tomorrow?" she asked, putting ice on a kitchen towel. She wrapped it up to use as an ice pack and went back to Jarod.

"What about it?" he asked, his eyes growing dark as she knelt down in front of him. She knew the feeling. However, she was in strict nurse mode at the moment.

"Will you be able to race?" she asked, reaching for his hand. "Look how swollen you are. This is all my fault. Again." She held his banged-up hand in hers and placed the ice pack on top. He flinched as the ice made contact with his torn knuckles.

"No." Jarod was adamant. "This was fucking Reddy's fault. But it's going to be fun tomorrow, let me tell you. NASCAR fans get off on fights. Contention of any kind is exciting, and this just raises the stakes."

"I don't like the sound of that." It was her turn to flinch. There was enough excitement on the track without adding to the drama. "You don't think he'll deliberately try to wreck your car, do you?"

"Sure." He shrugged. "If the idiot could ever catch me."

"Do you ever run out of that cockiness?" she asked, though she had to admit his confidence did make her feel more secure.

"I have no idea what you're talking about."

"That'd be a 'no' then," she said, keeping the ice pack on his hand as she stroked his arm.

"You could use some cockiness of your own, little girl," he said. "Now let's get rid of the ice so I can at least teach you how to defend yourself should you ever run into Big Red again."

"I don't believe in fighting." She stood up. "It's not in my nature."

"Such a delicate flower," he teased. "But I'm not buying it. I know there's a beast in there just waiting to be freed. Now get that sweet behind over here."

"Or what, you're going to grab it, like that disgusting asshole Reddy?"

"Don't remind me." He reached for her, snagged her hand, and pulled her onto his lap. "I *will* kill him if he ever lays a hand on you again. I promise you, he's going down tomorrow."

"Please, no." She rested her head on his chest, happy for the contact. "It's scary enough watching you out there without having to worry about you bumping cars."

"You worry?"

"Don't let it go to your head," she said, trying to keep things light. She didn't want him to know how much she worried. Or how much he'd come to mean to her over such a short time.

"Fine," he said, following her lead. "But I worry too, so let's get back to your self-defense lesson."

She agreed, happy for the distraction.

Over the next hour, Jarod held his own little fight club.

He taught her how to punch—the thumb goes on the *outside* of the fist, thank you very much—use her weight to bring someone down, and protect her face. She giggled through most of the tutorial.

"Vi, I hate to say it, but Red would've laid you out," he told her when she got too squirrely.

It was a sobering reality, so she began to take the rest of the lesson a little more seriously.

They covered the best way to distract an attacker (drop change on the ground—strange, but true), why it's important to be the first one to throw a punch if someone grabs you, and the location of all the high-value targets: eyes, ears, throat, groin, knees, and nose.

Jarod was oddly intense about the whole thing; she thought maybe it gave him the distraction he needed as well. Plus she did feel more empowered when they were done.

They finished the night with TV in her bed, and though he stayed with her the entire night, he didn't lay a hand on her.

Maybe he knew she was too emotional to handle it. Or maybe he thought she was scared from the fight. Either way, he opened his arms for her and she crawled in, and tried not to think about him driving with that maniac on the track tomorrow.

• • •

Qualifying day on race weekend meant they left early to work, but were home by dinnertime. It was usually Viv's favorite day: the excitement, the promise that anything could happen, and best of all—the way they spent the evening alone together.

Today, however, she was a basket case. She watched the track with complete concentration, squirming anytime Reddy came near Jarod's car.

Surprisingly, nothing happened. The entire day was uneventful. No brawls, bumps, accidents, or attitude on the track or off.

After racing for position during the day, Jarod went to the stands and signed autographs for the fans without being told. He was becoming someone she almost didn't recognize. But not in a bad way. He had finally let his guard down and was showing her—and his fans—more of himself.

She'd never been so proud, but she knew if she made a big deal out of it, he'd scoff. So after the press and fan activities, she walked with him back to the bus, keeping all her pride inside. Jarod kept his hand on her back the entire way. She liked his hand there, and even more, she liked the man at her side.

She couldn't believe she was actually happy to be back here in their little motor home village. Never one for camping, she did take a road trip with her family to the Grand Canyon one summer. This was a little like that. Traveling the summer in Jarod's bus.

So far they'd stayed in California, Nevada, Florida, Indiana, Tennessee, and now Virginia. Jarod had qualified for every race and finished in the top three for the majority of them. With just one month left, he was a shoo-in to quality for the ten-race Chase.

She went into the kitchen, and Jarod collapsed on the sofa in the living area. He turned on some soft music and closed his eyes. Viv learned this was his way to decompress after a race. Even though today was just a few laps for qualifying, it was still incredibly stressful. It unnerved her that she knew so much about his habits already.

"You want some tea?" She poured a tall glass because she already knew the answer.

"Please," he said, not opening his eyes.

She brought it to him along with a bowl of fruit. He usually liked to hydrate right after and only pick at something light, before devouring a meal an hour or so later, presumably after his body settled. Mrs. B packed her famous barbecue sandwiches, but Viv wanted to help, so Mrs. B gave her a recipe for baked cornmeal. It was similar to the cornbread Viv's mom served with chili, but with more fat. As everything seemed to be in this part of the country.

She sat on the couch next to Jarod and placed a large piece of a ripe peach up to his lips. "Here, I found a farmer's market on my walk this morning and picked these up."

Jarod sucked in the succulent fruit, not missing a beat to make her body melt. He swirled his tongue around her fingers in such a way, it made her wet. Like he had a direct connection to her core, whenever he pleased.

"Mmm," he growled. "Can I have another?"

He kept his eyes closed, making it easier for her to feed him without taking advantage of him. Once he looked at her in that way of his, she was usually toast.

She cut another piece and brought it to his lips. This time, as he took the fruit from her hands, he pulled her down onto the couch with him. Under him.

How she loved the sheer weight of his body. Warm and taut, his hips nestling perfectly between her legs. He fed her the piece of peach he held in his teeth before going in for a deep, invading kiss.

The juices dripped down her chin, but she didn't care. She had long given up being self-conscious around this man. Plus, he seemed to find everything she did sexy. He made her feel sexy regardless of what she was wearing or doing. That man could charm the panties off a nun.

As she was still floating from the kiss, Jarod managed to unbutton her blouse and was licking a path down her chest to her very tender nipples.

"Damn, you're sweet," he growled as he freed her breasts from the cups of her bra and took a long pull of each nipple. Viv tightened her thighs around his waist, pushing to get the friction she desperately craved.

He pulled away and looked at his watch. "This is not good," he said, and her stomach sank with the weight of a bag of bricks.

"What?"

"Charlie is having a barbecue soon, and I promised we'd be there." He raked a hand through his hair.

"Noooo," she cried.

His lips curved into that sexy half smile of his. "Don't worry, baby. I have about seven minutes and give or take thirty seconds before we have to get up and make ourselves presentable."

"Why aren't we presentable as we are?"

"We won't be after my seven minutes." He nestled back down and returned his attention to her aching breasts. This time, he pushed his erection directly on target. She groaned at the contact.

He rocked into her again. "Think I can get you off in under ten, baby?"

"Under five if you keep that up," she said.

She reached her arm back to the end table, where he kept a stack of condoms.

"Not going to need those for this round, babe."

And with that, he moved down her body, licking, sucking, and biting until he reached the waistband of her skirt. But instead of removing it, he simply bunched it up around her waist.

He pushed her panties to the side and took a long, appraising look. Her body burned, feeling more vulnerable this way than if he'd stripped her bare.

Lowering himself into position, she thought she heard him chuckle as he blew a long, hot gust of air across her center.

"God, you smell good, Vi," he said, inhaling her before making any contact.

It made her head swim, and she could feel the wetness all over the inside of her thighs.

"That's it," he said. "God, I love how wet you get."

She lifted slightly for him, and he released a sound that was more animal than human.

He placed his tongue at the very bottom of her opening, so dangerously close to the forbidden zone. She couldn't feel anything but the pressure of his tongue. He laved her, achingly slow, all the way up to her clit. She was so sensitive, she almost jumped when he used his tongue to circle the swollen nub. His hands slid under her bottom to bring her closer.

He closed his lips around that tight bundle of nerves and sucked so hard, she lost her breath.

"Jarod," she screamed, praying nobody heard her outside. There were always people milling about, so they never had the luxury of complete privacy.

He held her legs with one hand and slapped her bottom

with the other. The shock of it had her coming the very next second.

"Quiet," he scolded and went back to kissing her most private spot.

"Ahhh," she cried out again.

And again she received the burning sting of his hand.

His lips never left her quivering core, even when she tried to close her legs as the pressure proved too much to take. She reached her arms above her head, grasping for the edge of the sofa. Something to hold on to, something to pull herself away, just for a moment of relief.

Jarod wasn't having it, but he did place a wet kiss on her belly, giving her the reprieve she needed, and then reached up for her hands, locking his grip around her wrists. Resuming his position, he placed her hands in his wild mass of hair.

"Here, baby," he said. "You can be in control now. Direct me anyway you want it. As rough as you want. Don't be shy."

He never ceased to amaze and surprise her.

Viv let her hands wander through his glorious head of hair while he pleasured her. She pulled him up a little so she could feel the rough stubble of his jaw on the insides of her thighs, over her throbbing center. Oh God, that was it.

He consumed her then, allowing her to tighten her thighs around his head, and she held on while he thrust his tongue in and out of her. It was so incredibly intimate. So dirty. Her skirt around her waist and all his sandy hair moving around between her legs. She couldn't tear her eyes away.

Jarod groaned as he devoured her, and it sent vibrations deep into her bones. Her inner walls tightened. She began quaking from the inside out as a powerful orgasm shuddered though her, rendering her completely immobile. The aftermath left her loose and pliant, floating in a sea of ecstasy. Her bones liquefied; her brain went numb.

But it wasn't just her body. Her heart throbbed inside her chest, and she had to fight back tears. What the hell? She'd heard about women who cried during orgasm, though she never quite believed it. Sounded too sappy and contrived.

She understood now. The emotion was so intense she thought she was going to rip open.

Jarod righted her clothes, treating her with so much care. Once she was pulled back together, he settled her on his lap and kissed her head.

"That was the most beautiful thing I've even seen." He wrapped her in his arms.

Viv leaned into his embrace wanting to say something, to tell him something. Did he know how she was feeling? Could he tell?

He checked his watch and shot his arms in the air, taking Viv out of her blissed-out state and into the real world. "Two minutes to spare," he exclaimed.

She laughed. She couldn't let him know there'd been a major development in those last five minutes.

Something had happened, and she didn't know what to make of it. But one thing was clear: Jarod didn't feel the same way. So she was going to have to check that shit at the door and not let him see it.

Crying during an orgasm. Really, really*?*

Still, she couldn't help but wonder, what if he did feel the same way?

PR Rule Number 9: Never show your cards.

So Viv gave him a quick peck on the cheek and went to her room to get ready for the evening.

Chapter Seventeen

The last place Jarod wanted to be right now was with a bunch of oil-stained guys with dirty fingernails, when Viv had just rocked his goddamn world. No. He wanted to stay right where he was in their little bus, hogging her all to himself.

He had never been the sort of guy to take without giving in bed. He enjoyed getting his woman off almost as much as getting himself off. Almost.

Until the stubborn Yank came into his life and turned everything upside-down.

He would forgo pleasure anytime to take care of her. Making her come apart, opening her up. Taking down all her defenses and laying her bare before him was right up there with being the first to cross a finish line in a race. Of course, the sex was beyond compare as well, but what had just happened in the bus? It transcended the physical.

Hell, now he sounded like those meditation books she liked to read. Yes, he paged through a few when he was in her room. He'd go in there sometimes when she was working and he had a second of downtime. Would go in there just to catch her scent—in the light of day. Fuck all. He was out of control for this girl.

Yet he knew nothing serious could happen. They had one month left together, and then she'd be on her way to New York, and he'd be closer than he ever had been to the prize he'd been waiting his whole life for. That's what was important. And that's what he needed to remember.

This was a little make-believe life they were playing at right now. Hell, Vi was absolutely forced into it. Practically threatened by her boss. She was just making the best of it because that's what she did. She never felt sorry for herself; she didn't want to be pitied. She made a plan and stuck the fuck to it.

He could learn a thing or two from that.

She came out of her room wearing a simple tank top and jeans.

Shit, he liked it better when he didn't have a plan and could let his dick make most of his decisions.

But it was too late for that. One month. Then they'd both be off to bigger and better things. And if he planned to win the Sprint Cup, he'd be doing it without her. So he needed to friggin' man up and keep his distance. Not an easy task, especially when she looked the way she did in those jeans. The way they hugged her curved hips—that she desperately tried to keep as slim as possible. Sure she teased him about his diet, but the girl ate like a bird. He'd actually like to see how they looked filled out a little more. Did she let herself put on a few pounds over the holidays? Did she ever indulge?

His heart squeezed, knowing he wouldn't be around to find out the answer.

"Ready?" she asked, taking a step toward him and clouding his head with her wildflower scent.

"Sure," he said stiffly, leading her to the door.

"Oooh." She stopped them. "Just a sec." She went into the kitchen and grabbed a bread basket off the counter.

She reached under the towel that covered the basket and pulled out a piece of cornbread.

He opened his mouth for a taste and was instantly taken back home.

"Christ," he said, and leaned in for another bite. "How did you…?"

"Mrs. B gave me your mother's recipe. I thought I'd serve it with the pork tonight, but since we're going out, I thought I'd bring it with. Can't go to a party empty-handed, right? That'd be *rude*." She said it in the dramatic, smart-ass way that was all Viv.

"So the Yank is finally learning."

"*Pffft.*" She blew him off. "I guess it's the least I could do after your little gift to me on the couch."

"Oh yeah?" he asked.

"Yeah," Viv said, this time looking a little shy.

"Well, let me tell you, baby." He met her eyes. "That was just as much a gift to myself. The gift that keeps on giving."

"And, he ruins it," she said with a smile, but he thought there might actually be some truth to those words.

"Aww," he said, reaching for his old standby. "You know you love it."

Yep. Officially screwed.

There was no way he'd deny them when it came right

down to it, he knew that. It didn't help anyone to put up such unrealistic expectations, but it had to be limited and not so fucking emotional. It was time to develop a backup plan. Fun. Easy. That was the new name of the game.

Yes, it was time to rebuild those walls.

• • •

Once they left the lust-filled bus, it was easier to breathe. There was a surprisingly nice breeze for Virginia in August. The sun sat low in the sky and caught Viv's hair, showing off the golds and auburns mixed in with the chestnut and chocolate. Yes, he could probably spout poetry about her hair, and her legs, and write an entire goddamn book about that heavenly place between her thighs. Ch-rist, he had it bad.

The press and suits were gone and it was just *them* in the lot: the drivers and crew. That's how Jarod often looked at it: *us* versus *them*. The press had shut down for the day, and the fans had dispersed. All the interviews and tagalongs and sponsorship events were over for the time being.

It was just the racing family.

This was what Jarod loved most.

When he was a kid, this was the time when his dad was just his dad. They were the stolen moments. They'd have barbecues like the one the Stewarts were throwing tonight. Usually, his mother hosted them. It was an amazing way to grow up. Riding around in golf carts with his friends, jumping from bus to bus. His mama even took Jarod and Kate to a makeshift church in the infield.

"Hey y'all," Charlie's wife, Alisha, greeted them in the imaginary front yard of their bus. The Stewarts did it up right.

They had chairs out front, a long table where drivers from at least six states represented their version of barbecue. Sorry, saps. Everyone knew that South Carolina's was the best—as Alisha would attest.

"Thank the Lord, someone who knows how barbecue is done right," she said, wrapping her arms around Jarod. He gave her a hearty squeeze. "And you must be Vivian." She held a hand out to his very nervous-looking, what would he call her, friend? Lover? Spin doctor? Hookup? None seemed to fit. Thankfully, Alisha knew not to make him put her in a category.

"Thanks for having us," Vi said, stiff as all hell.

"You never need an invitation," Alisha said. "Our door is always open."

As if on cue, almost a dozen kids came scrambling out of the Stewarts' bus and practically knocked Viv down in the process.

She just laughed. Her smile lit up her eyes—that was his second-favorite expression on her. The first, hands down, was how she looked on his couch.

Jarod cleared his throat and tried to shake away the image.

Jesus, just let me have the night without wanting to defile that woman.

"Those monsters, however, are a different story," Alisha said. "Kids, grab a plate and then head up to the rooftop. There's a table set up there for you. We'd like to eat in peace for a change."

"I have some cornbread," Viv said, a little more subdued than her take-charge self. "Where would you like me to put it?"

"Anywhere on the table, hon," Alisha said. "Charlie's been in charge of arranging that food, so God only knows what he has going on over there. It looks delish, by the way. Homemade, right?"

Viv nodded, and Jarod thought he could see a trace of pride there.

"I haven't had cornbread that doesn't come from a box in ages. Now what can I get you two to drink? I know Mr. Clean will have water, but can I temp you, Viv? I have some sangria inside."

"Love some," Viv said, moving over to the table to drop off her cornbread.

Jarod watched as she moved a few things to make room, knowing full well what was about to happen.

She stared at the table, wide-eyed, then her busy hands shifted into action. A minute later, she slapped her hands together. "All done. This setup should make dinner a little smoother."

He'd watched her reorganize the entire table, even orienting all of the serving spoons to the right. "Just couldn't help yourself, could you?"

Alisha came out with a drink for Vi and stole her away for the next hour with the other WAGs, along with a few other NASCAR fixtures like Kelsey and a couple gals in hospitality. In this group, the ladies were the real deal, just as much a part of the team as the crew. And they could detect a pit lizard or bullshitter a mile away. Viv fit right in.

Don't even go there, Cage. This is only temporary.

"I think you got a real good one there," Charlie said as Jarod finished the best ribs of his life. "Though I never thought I'd see you fall for a Northern gal with your stubborn

Southern ways."

"No," Jarod said. "It's not like that. She's just working, trying to save my hide from being kicked off the circuit. And what do you mean my stubborn ways?"

"Dude, you always have to be sweet-talked. No one can ever give it to you straight. Come on. How do you think it is that Gina's been able to manipulate you for so long? You like to just let things go. But I bet that doesn't fly with Viv over there, does it?"

"Like I said, what I have with Viv is a working relationship."

"You sure?" he asked. "The two of you have been joined at the hip for weeks. Doing your little exercises in the mornings? Hiding away in your bus at night?"

"Spying on us, dude?" Jarod said. "That's low."

"You know that's just how it is 'round here. Too easy to be up in everyone's business. And word on the street is that you've got it bad for that girl."

"Even if that's what I wanted—which I don't—it's not a possibility. She's heading to New York in a month. And I'll be on my way to the Chase."

"If you say so, but you better watch out, Cage, because I'm hot on your tail."

Jarod shot the shit with his buddies, whom he never forgot were also his competitors once the green flag dropped.

But when the women joined them, it was even better. Viv listened so intently to their stories and asked questions about the drivers and the races. She even snooped into Jarod's life in a sweet way. And she was the perfect sport when the guys asked her about her freakiest clients. Viv remained professional and didn't give out any names, but she did leak a few very juicy tidbits about a celebrity or two.

"Why didn't you tell me your handler, Kelsey, is Kelsey Rider, Bobby's daughter?" Vi said, when she stole him away for a moment alone, back behind the Stewarts' bus.

Jarod was more than disappointed that she brought him back here for an inquiry, when he thought maybe she wanted to get a little somethin'-somethin'. Lord knows he sure did.

He scratched the scruff on his chin, playing coy. He'd have his fun with her one way or another. "The bigger question is, did you know who Bobby Rider was before the WAGs told you?"

"Yes," she said, indignant, lifting her chin up. A move that made him want to kiss her senseless. "I know he's a racing legend, and that he raced with your dad."

"Hmmm." He nodded. "Impressive."

"I just can't believe you didn't tell me." She bumped her shoulder with his. Odd. Why was this so interesting to her? She dealt with famous people all the time.

"Not my place," he answered, but he was intrigued now. "Plus she doesn't like the attention."

"Sounds like someone else I know." Vi raised a brow.

"We had a similar upbringing," he said. "That's for sure. Kelsey and my sister, Kate, were inseparable." Actually, the three of them were, despite the six-year age difference. There weren't many kids who grew up on the track, or who had fathers who risked their lives every weekend. They all had a special bond. Still did. Hanging with Kels on race weekends was like hanging with family. And he trusted her immensely.

"Your sister and Kelsey are friends?" Vi asked, positively giddy.

"All right woman, what's going on here? Why are we even talking about this? And why are you so…invested?"

He backed her up against the Stewarts' bus.

"I'm invested, not, you know, *invested*." She tripped on her words. "It's just that I thought Kelsey hated me and was trying to undermine my work."

"Why the hell would you think that?"

"Well," Vi said, busy drawing designs in the dirt with the toe of her shoe. "Because she was always so happy to see you and smirked whenever she saw the two of us together, I thought she…wanted you."

"Ohhh." He scrunched up his face and tried to shake away the image. Kelsey was like a sister to him.

"Okay." Viv clapped. "So I have nothing to worry about then." She smiled and grabbed his hand, officially ending the conversation by walking them back to the party before he had the chance to make sense of what just happened.

Nothing to worry about, she told him.

He wouldn't make any promises.

• • •

Once the sun set, Charlie brought out his guitar. He loved playing, but even more, he loved a gentle reminder to the guys who had had a bit too much to drink that it was time to slow it down.

Couples filled the space in front of the Stewarts' bus and slow danced as Charlie quietly sang a Blake Shelton ballad.

Jarod held out a hand to Viv, who shook her head. Never wanting to let go, her initial impulse was already to shut down any fun. But as Jarod had discovered, all it took was a gentle touch to change her mind.

He stood up and placed his hand on hers, coaxing her

out of her seat, and in the next moment she was in his arms, and he was enclosed in the sweet and warm bubble that was all Vivian Blake.

Jarod led her in a slow and close two-step, and she fell into pace with him perfectly. With her tucked into the crook of his neck, he met Charlie's eyes. The bastard raised his brow, all-knowingly. Jarod flipped him off.

Then the smart-ass played a song called "New York City Girl."

"May I cut in?" A voice pulled him out of the bubble.

Aw, hell no.

"No," Jarod said without any trace of manners, tightening his grip.

Viv looked up at Lach, and Jarod swore her heart sped up. All the pit lizards called him Melbourne Ken—instead of Malibu Ken. He looked like a plastic doll, all right. And acted just as fake. Didn't stop the women from hanging on his every word. Not that he cared. He knew it was the damn Aussie accent anyway.

"Jarod." Viv laughed uncomfortably. "Don't be so rude."

"Right, mate," Lach said. "Listen to the lady."

Jarod reluctantly released her to make introductions. "Vi, this is Lachlan Walker. King of the unnecessary bump-draft and royal pain in my ass."

"Right." Lach leveled a look at him. "But don't forget to mention, that bump got you to first place, you dumb bloke."

"Nice to meet you, Lachlan," Viv said, clearly trying to diffuse the situation beginning to brew. "I'm Viv Blake."

"Pleasure is mine," he said, taking Viv's hand, pulling her into a dance.

Jarod went to the corner to brood while another man

danced with his woman. Fuck, he didn't mean to think that. His palms itched with each slow two-step the asshole made. His jaw clenched as he waited out the painfully long song.

Shit, when was it going to end?

After the dance was finally over, the three of them sat down in the lawn chairs to the left of the food. Little Naomi jumped onto her dad's lap.

"Hey, love," Lach said. "Meet my new lady friend, Vivian."

"You have a lot of lady friends, Daddy." The little girl giggled. She was the only reason Jarod remained civil with the guy. Lach's wife left him (and Naomi) a few years ago without so much as a note.

"Well," Lach said, "this lady is very special. She's with Mr. Cage."

Jarod knew the bastard said that just to put him on the spot with Vi, but he wasn't going to correct him. Turns out, Vi didn't either.

"Nice to meet you." Viv smiled. "What's your name?"

"Naomi." She jumped up and twirled in her bright yellow dress.

"Beautiful name," Vi said, clearly charmed by the girl. That wasn't unusual, Naomi was adorable.

The little girl entertained them all, dancing to Charlie's songs and taking turns pulling each of them onto the makeshift dance floor. They moved under Alisha's twinkling lights, which hung off the awning of the Stewarts' bus, to country tear-jerkers and bouncy pop songs. Naomi requested Taylor Swift several times, and Charlie obliged.

When Vi wasn't on the dance floor or off discussing nail polish colors (and Lord knows what else) with Naomi, she stayed close to his side. She'd come to fit into his world with ease, and he was actually able to relax for a few hours—even Lach didn't seem as annoying as usual.

Too soon, his friend played the final tune for the night. This time, Jarod didn't let anyone cut in on his last dance with his PR manager—who was quickly coming to mean a whole helluva lot more to him.

Chapter Eighteen

Viv didn't say much on their walk back to Jarod's bus. Secretly, she didn't want to ruin the perfect night.

"So was that terrible for you?" he asked as they both took off their shoes and curled up on the couch. "The race talk all night?"

"Not at all," she said. "I had a great time."

"And Lach?"

"What about him?"

"He didn't get you all hot and bothered with that accent, and the good manners, and that ridiculous surfer hair, did he?"

"Not really," she said, playing with him, just a little. "I mean, I do love an accent."

"Oh you do, do you?" He pulled her legs across his lap so he could massage her feet.

Her breath caught, and she realized she wasn't in the mood for games.

"Yes," she answered. "But I prefer accents of a Southern variety."

"Music to my ears," he said, bringing her foot to his mouth, kissing and nipping on her arch.

"And also," she said, hoping to seal the deal, "I've never been attracted to the surfer type. I prefer rugged men with unruly hair…and a filthy mouth."

She didn't get a chance to see his expression, because the very next second she was cradled in his arms and he was walking toward the bedroom.

"I hate to disappoint you, baby," Jarod said when he placed her on the bed. "But I'm not going to talk dirty tonight. I'm not going to be doing much talking at all."

Strange, but his words had the same effect on her that they always did. She warmed and ached and throbbed for him all at once. But more than anything, she wanted his lips on her.

He rolled with her on the bed, pinning her under his weight. He kissed her slowly, with a closed mouth at first, as if he was savoring each taste. Parting her lips with his tongue, he unleashed the kind of kiss that made her limbs go boneless—his hand holding her chin while his mouth captured hers.

His eyes locked on hers for a moment. Usually this was where he'd start talking, turning her on so much with his naughty promises that she was begging for it.

Turns out he didn't have to use the words, and she didn't have to beg for it.

They took their time undressing each other like they'd been lovers for years. No hurry, no fumbling. It was slow and easy, and Viv never felt more wanted in her life.

He touched her so thoroughly, he left no part of her unmarked, and she did the same. Claiming him with each touch. He reached for a condom, but she was the one to cover him.

And when he sank into her, he whispered her name.

Viv had to hold in the tears. Why? She didn't understand, but her sex life with Jarod had become so consuming and emotional, it was hard to control her responses to him.

She didn't get the chance to think about it, because he started to move—slow and deep, driving them into that blissful state she'd experienced only with him. She soared higher and higher until there nothing was left to tether her to the ground. She was floating.

Jarod was right there, his fingers interlaced with hers.

When they drifted back down to earth, neither of them bothered moving from the tangle they wrapped themselves in. Instead, they let exhaustion pull them under.

The next morning, she was quiet when she woke. Jarod was still snuggled up against her, and she didn't want to disturb the fantasy going on in her head about making their current status permanent.

If Jarod won the Sprint Cup, he honestly could use someone full-time to handle all of his PR and charity work. She could even start a nonprofit in his name so he could give back in his own way, without having to adhere to someone else's rules.

So what if it wasn't her dream job? Jarod was turning out to be more than the dream guy for her. They could make it work. It would be a quieter life than what Viv was used to, but maybe that was a good thing. She loved Cotton Creek. Really loved it, especially after the past few hellish months at Elite. She loved having the downtime. The juggling back and forth. The contrast that always appealed to her so much.

The question was, did he feel the same way?

• • •

Later that day, that answer was perfectly clear. Viv had to find out from Henry and crew that this was the track that killed Jarod's dad. He didn't mention it when they'd arrived. Before qualifying. Or at any time over the past three days when they were in bed or when they were out. After all they'd been through, he didn't trust her enough to talk about it.

She worked with the media all morning on the upcoming interviews, knowing he wasn't going to cooperate this weekend. She tried to make excuses for him, but was bombarded with insulting questions about why he wouldn't discuss his dad.

The comments had her mama bear instincts on high alert. Her business sense, however, seemed to be shut down for the day.

And when Jarod's nemesis cornered her in the pressroom, all hell broke loose.

"So, is J.C. trying to break the General's record on the track today?" Brooks asked. "We haven't seen him."

"He's been swamped today, guys," she said, covering for her client. "Another charity event this morning."

"That's nice," Brooks said. "But what might've been even nicer was if he showed up for the memorial for his father today. The one they have every year. Do you know he's never attended? Not once. Sometimes I think the fans care more about his passing than his only son."

And that's when Viv's mouth started moving before her brain turned on.

"Oh really, Brooks," she spat. "Is that what you think? Because, hell, I'm sure you of all people would know. Just as I'm sure you know that Jarod marks this day and his time at this track on his own each and every time he's here. I'm sure you also know that Jarod has his father's number tattooed on his leg, right?"

The room quieted, cameras turned on. And a crowd started to gather, but Viv was too far gone to notice.

"And that the entire Cage family says a prayer together the morning he arrives here. I bet you know that. What about the photo of his father that he carries in his chest pocket, you know about that too, right?"

Viv didn't remember much more than that, other than storming out of there. Only to encounter something much, much worse.

• • •

"You had no right to do that, Viv," Jarod snarled after the qualifying race. He wouldn't talk to her before he hit the track. It was the first time she'd seen Jarod irate. She had a taste the first day they met. But his mood that day had nothing on this thunderstorm.

"I'm just doing my job, Jarod." She crossed her arms. "Brooks was trying to bury you."

"You should've let him."

"Stop telling me how to do my job," she said. "I was trying to protect you. And I went into this situation cold.

You could've told me about everything that goes on for your father's memorial. How can I do my job when you keep things from me?"

"Remember who you're working for," he warned.

He stepped closer, trying to intimidate her. She pushed him away.

"I don't fucking care anymore." She pounded his chest with her fist. "I have a job to do here, and I'm damn well going to do it."

The crowd around them quickly cleared out, and soon they had the garage to themselves.

She almost hated him in that moment. Hated that he made her look like a blubbering idiot. An emotional woman who couldn't handle a man like Jarod Cage.

But when her nipples peaked under her shirt, she knew she couldn't convince the rest of her body that he was an overbearing asshole. She was his…and they both knew it.

He caught a glimpse of her shirt, and his eyes went dark. Then he grabbed her by the wrists and dragged her into the secluded area of the garage, just as he did in Atlanta all those weeks ago.

"I will not tolerate you talking to me like that in front of my crew." He was shaking, he was so mad or so horny. It was hard to tell, and Viv would be lying if she didn't admit she was scared shitless and turned on beyond measure all at the same time.

"And you will not belittle the work I'm doing here," she said, not backing down.

"You are infuriating." He backed her against the car.

"No more than you, my friend."

"We are not friends," he said, flipping her away from him

and leaning over her so she had no choice but to brace her hands on the hood of the car. He unbuckled her linen trousers so they pooled at her ankles, drawing her panties down with them.

She could feel his heavy erection between her cheeks, but she wasn't about to let him know it excited her.

"Does that feel like we're friends?" he asked.

She reached back and palmed him over his fire suit, gripping him tightly before she started to stroke.

She turned to face him, because if this was going to happen, if he wanted a hate fuck, he was going to know exactly who was giving it to him.

She knew she shouldn't. If she gave in. If she showed him everything. If she offered it all and he said no, how could she possibly recover? Even worse? What if he said yes?

He pulled her so tight, not even daylight could pass between them.

The pulse in his jaw kept time to the thump of her heart, both faster than they should've been.

Two could play at his game, and he was not going to win this time. Bypassing the point of no return, without even slowing down to be sure, Viv placed his hand between her legs.

She pushed a single finger on top of his, drawing a line down her seam, through the wetness he had to know was waiting for him.

"Does this feel like friends?" she countered, resisting her need to take that finger deeper.

"No," Jarod admitted, the traces of anger dissolving right before her eyes. "It feels like more."

"I don't believe you," she said, opening the fly to his suit to release his heavy erection. "All you want is a *yes girl*."

"If that was true, I sure as fuck wouldn't be with you, Vi," he said, moving that lone finger. "I think all you want is to finish this job so you can land that cushy spot in New York. It's not about what's best for me. It's about what's best for you."

His words hurt, maybe because there was some truth to them. But he had to know she'd never sacrifice him to look good to the press. "That's not true," she said, determined to prove it.

"Show me then," he pleaded, before he crushed his lips into hers.

She opened for him, and he took her deep as he fused their mouths together, consuming her. His tongue had the faint taste of mint, and he smelled like his signature citrus scent mixed with oil and sweat—it was a heady aroma that pushed her over the edge.

"Back to the bus," he growled, but Viv wasn't about to let that happen. She couldn't handle soft and sweet and meaningful. She wouldn't.

"No," she said before dropping to her knees. She would show him what he meant to her now. How she'd do anything for him. Even now, she wanted him to use her, sick as it was. She wanted his dirty mouth and rough hands all over her. She didn't want to have to think about anything other than this moment.

She wasted no time on seduction. No teasing touches or swirl of her tongue. She simply opened her mouth and waited.

"Shit, baby," he groaned. "What the hell game are you playing?"

She did nothing but look up…and wait.

That did it.

He took his weighty cock and guided it to her mouth. She looked on as he pushed inside her inch by beautiful inch.

"Look at me," he demanded. "If this is how you want it, I want to see those doe eyes looking up at me."

She met his eyes, her mouth full of him now. She could feel his length tickling the back of her throat.

He began rocking his hips, slowly, methodically, and took her under. It was exactly where she wanted to be. His breath grew shallow and louder, louder, until he pulled out of her mouth and hauled her back to her feet. He gripped her leg and wrapped it around his waist, but she struggled. She couldn't be with him face-to-face, not now. He would see her and know what this meant to her. It was too risky.

Instead, she brought her leg down and turned her back to him, right where they started.

"If that's the only way I can have you," he said, pushing her chest down on the hood of the car, "you know I'm going to take it."

She couldn't prepare for what happened next.

He ripped open a condom wrapper, holding her in place. Then in one sharp and brutal thrust, he was completely buried inside. A punishing move for her distance. She didn't care. She wanted to be punished.

He drove into her. Over and over again. She not only took it, she reared back and met him for each demanding drive. Her legs began to shake, and she knew there was no stopping it now. There was nothing left but pleasure, no room for anything else as they both reached the climax together before crashing down.

Chapter Nineteen

Jarod was more pissed now than when he heard what she did with the media. How dare she mess with his feelings and desire for her. Reduce him to some sort of animal that kicks out his crew and fucks his woman in a goddamn garage.

He was more than this, and she knew it. But she didn't care, and it seemed like the worst kind of betrayal after all they shared together.

After putting himself back together, he helped her with her clothes.

"Well, that was fun," she said, trying to make light of the situation.

Trouble was, he didn't do light.

He ignored her and said, "I'm going back to the bus. I need to get some rest before tomorrow."

"Okay," she said. He knew she wouldn't push. This was how it was going to be now. They got as close as they were physically able, but emotionally, she was a locked vault, and she wasn't opening for anyone. Least of all him. "I'll just take a walk before I turn in."

He watched her leave before he headed toward the bus, an empty feeling hollowing out his insides.

Once he was in the safety of his temporary home, he locked himself in the bathroom. He ran a shower out of habit. She was just like the rest of them. Water pounded over his head, his tired muscles, washing away her scent. The more he thought about her rejection, the more his stomach churned. At this point, it was making him feel physically ill. Bottom line was she wanted something from him, and when it no longer suited her, she'd cut and run.

For once in his life, he'd tried to be real, but she couldn't handle it. Didn't want it or him.

He never drank before a race, but one time wasn't going to kill him. He'd hit up one of the crew guys, kick back a couple, and try to forget about her for the night.

Still, he looked for her in the lot, unable to help himself worrying about her out her alone in the dark.

• • •

Jarod found the guys and managed to put more than a few down before stumbling into Gina on his way back to the bus. Of all the luck.

"Well, look who it is," Jarod said, his voice rich in sarcasm. "My lovely fiancée." Really, he was surprised she hadn't shown up sooner. But then from what he'd seen on ESPN, she was moving up the ranks, covering more than the just the X-Game type sports, and expanding beyond the motocross world. Well, effing goody for her.

"Hi," she said, making her way to him. When she did, she waved a hand over her nose. "Whoa, have you been drinking before the race?"

"What's it to you?" Christ, his mouth felt like it was full of cotton balls.

"Nothing," she said, teetering on her heels as they sank into the dirt. "Just want to be sure you're taking care of yourself."

"Right." He laughed.

"I am glad I ran into you, though." She lowered her voice when some of Charlie's crewmen walked by. "I have something I want to discuss. A little favor. This is the last one, I promise."

"What do you want, Gina?"

She tilted her head in a way that used to drive him crazy. Her black glossy hair falling over her shoulder. Her tight little dress, highlighting her ample cleavage. Man, he used to have it bad for her. But now? Nothing. She couldn't hold a candle to all the class and brains and beauty (inside and out) that was Vivian. There was no contest.

"I have a business proposition for you." Gina pushed out her chest in what he knew was an effort to distract him. It didn't work.

"No," he said, cutting her off.

"Just for show to give us both a PR bump, J." She pouted. Oh, she was bringing out all the stops tonight. "I was thinking we should get back together publicly. Until you get to the Chase."

He glanced around the quiet rows of motor homes, feeling like he was on one of those hidden camera shows. Really, just when he'd thought his day couldn't get any worse…

"Isn't that what you've already had people believing?" he asked. "What do you need me for?"

"Proof," she said, waving her phone. "Photos I can put on social media. They won't believe anything I have to say unless we're seen together. My ratings went sky-high after Bathroom Gate, but things are starting to level out."

The thought of her profiting from his near-disaster pissed him off. Especially since her comments compounded the shitstorm he was in. "If it gave you such a good bump, why did you threaten my favorite body parts when it happened?"

"I had no idea the public would rally around me like they did." She smiled, clearly delighted by that fact. "I thought your dirt would be sticky, but as it turned out, it just made me more lovable."

"So glad it worked out for you."

"It worked for you, too," she said. "You're doing great now. World-class spin doctor working every angle. Baby, you'd even be welcome at church these days. And a reunion of racing's golden couple would elevate the good PR to a new level. Good for you, good for me."

He heaved a sigh. Damn it, he was tired. So damn tired of it all. "And then what?"

"Then, once you get to the Chase and I become irreplaceable at the network, we can announce an amicable split." She steepled her hands like it was the most obvious plan ever. Like it wasn't his life, his entire future, or the jobs of more than a dozen people hanging on the line of public opinion. And worse, here was another woman out to take what she wanted from him and leave him high and dry when she was finished. His relationship with Gina had always been tenuous at best, but he hadn't thought her this heartless.

"Haven't I paid you back enough yet?" he said. "Fuck, Gina, I can't take much more of the circus. You know that. I thought through all of this we finally became friends."

"We have, J." She hugged him. She actually fucking hugged him. "This is it. I promise you. It's been years since the accident, and I've never leaked a thing. The story of your dad taking prescription pills before the accident would've made my career. You know that, right?"

"It also would've destroyed my family." His head began to throb—he couldn't go into this tonight.

"Which is why I've protected you." She rubbed his shoulders to soothe, but her touch only made his skin crawl. "Yes, I had to ask for something in return. But now, I actually have pull with the media and I have more to offer you. And let's face it, you know you'll be in trouble sooner or later, especially when you don't have the fancy PR chick on payroll. When that time comes, I'll be there to help you. What do you say?"

Jarod knew it was the worst possible idea, but she was right. Vi would be gone soon enough, and he needed to bank some goodwill.

Chapter Twenty

They wouldn't recover from this, Viv knew that now. Jarod had let so few people in, and there was a reason why. He was a paycheck for so many, a stop on their way someplace else. Viv was just as guilty of jumping aboard the J-train and jumping off when things got a little complicated. When he showed his true colors.

While he loved the dirty talking in bed, almost as much as Viv loved hearing it, it was a wall he built up to protect himself. And it was heartbreaking.

Viv's head pounded; she needed coffee like yesterday. She'd hardly slept last night, even after her long walk. All she could think about was the damage she'd done. That's why she couldn't distinguish the difference between the buzz in her head and the buzzing of her phone.

Perfect. Just what she needed.

Miranda.

"I assume you've read *Race Way*, then?" she said by way

of greeting.

The one thing good about being on Jarod's payroll, maybe the only good thing now, was the distance it kept Viv from the Ice Queen.

She looked at her clock: 6:00 a.m.

"Just getting to my office now, Miranda."

Silence.

Viv woke up her mouse from its slumber and clicked on the bookmark. Yes, Miranda did have some good ideas.

And there it was.

A photo of Jarod and his ex. The caption read: *Jarod Cage has midnight powwow with racing princess. We smell reconciliation…*

No, no, no, no. How could the bastard do that? Just an hour after she let him have his way with her in the garage.

This couldn't be happening. Was he really back together with the *racing princess*?

Viv cleared her throat.

"I don't know whether it's true or not," Miranda said in a voice Viv didn't recognize, snapping her out of her nightmare. "I don't care. This is brilliant. If Gina can forgive him, anyone can. This is very good for him. For us. Good work, Viv."

"Um, ah…" Viv struggled to find the words, but it was too late. Miranda had already hung up.

Viv went out to the living room to find Jarod crashed out on the couch. The air was full of stale beer, pizza, and quite possibly Southern Comfort. She'd never forget that smell after rush week in college. What the hell happened to him? He never drank before a race. Never.

The bigger person would wake him gently and ask what

happened. The strong businesswoman would make a pot of coffee and her famous hangover cure-all breakfast to get him right for the day's race. But she was neither. She was an irrational, scorned woman. So she flipped on the lights, blasted the TV, and left the motor coach for the nearest greasy spoon, because serving up grits was her only career option after this debacle.

How could she possibly work with him now?

The fact that the move was helping his image made her cry for the fifth time that morning. If the comments on the article were in line with the rest of the racing fans out there, Jarod Cage was well on his way into the bosom of the public. And Gina would giggle her way to the top of sports reporting. Win. Fucking. Win.

• • •

What in the fresh hell is this torture?

Jarod woke up to a blasting TV and bright lights. His head ached and stomach heaved, and he was fairly certain something had died in his mouth.

It didn't take long to remember what had happened to put him in such a state. First, the nightmare with Vi, and then the big kahuna of all paybacks, his final trade-off with Gina.

Fuck, did Vi know?

Judging from her empty room, the blaring TV, and the empty coffeepot, she'd most definitely heard.

Shit, he had to find her.

After a quick shower and a gallon of coffee, Jarod pulled himself together. He'd done so much press the day before, his little Yank gave him a break today. He was only on tap for a few fan events. Of course there'd be some reporters dying to get a comment about the Gina situation. Though she had assured him she'd be able to keep most of them off his back for a while. She'd do the talking. Of course Gina would. She was all about the publicity for herself and raking in as much media time as she could.

Viv met Jarod for his first fan signing. She looked wrecked, and he couldn't believe that this was the exact reaction he was hoping for last night.

"Hey, about last night," he said, under his breath.

"Don't worry about it," she said, painting on a smile. "I think I'm up to speed on the news of the day and don't worry, it won't impact our arrangement. I will help get you to the Chase. Not that you need my help anymore. The move with Gina was brilliant. I wish I would've thought of it."

"Not real," he said, unable to say anymore.

"None of it is," Viv replied, before the fans made their way in.

The day went by in a blur, and each time he tried to get Vi's attention, she threw more business at him.

Jarod was not an overly superstitious man, for a race car driver anyway, but there were bad omens all over. First, a fight with a woman was a terrible way to go into a race. Second, Vi was wearing green, which happened to be the worst color in racing due to the number of fatal car wrecks in green cars. For some reason, he thought that might have been on purpose on her part. All she needed to do now was start eating peanuts—also an omen for car crashes.

As he prepared for the race, he was about as low as a guy could go. There was no secret kiss from Viv. No message from his fake fiancée. Shit, even his mom forgot to call him.

No, that wasn't true. She never called before a race. Still, he never felt more alone.

So Jarod patted the photo in his chest pocket, said a prayer, and raced the best he could under the circumstances.

He came in eighth. Not what he was hoping for, but it could've been so much worse.

After the race, Vi informed him she'd be hitching a ride in the Stewarts' jet, because they also lived in Atlanta. She'd be in touch by email and would see him at the Pennsylvania 400.

Those next four days were the longest of his life.

Chapter Twenty-One

Viv stayed on the down low. Since she'd been crashing with Jarod during the home days, she knew it would seem suspicious if she went into the office. She also couldn't take dealing with Miranda right now, so she locked herself inside her apartment and sulked.

Someone, however, knew exactly where she'd been.

In a large envelope left on her doorstep were photos of her and Jarod in the most compromising positions.

No, this wasn't happening. She almost got him to the Chase, and she almost had her New York position in the bag. It couldn't end this way—in some sleazy scandal. She wouldn't let that happen. To either of them.

She turned to the only person she trusted, punching in her number as fast as she could.

"Thank God," Viv said when Mel answered. "I need help. Stat."

"Where are you?" Mel questioned. Viv hadn't had a

chance to fill her in about Gina, or the sex, or the fact that she committed the ultimate sin and fell ass-over-teapot for the Wheelman. Yup, she might as well admit it, she'd been *Caged*.

"Home," Viv answered.

"On my way," Mel said. It was the only information her friend needed.

Viv curled up on her cold sofa, flipping through the pictures, over and over again, until Mel arrived.

Mel took a seat next to Viv and studied the photos for a long time, not saying a word. Completely unlike her. This was bad. It was so bad. Viv didn't remember that she was fighting with the man and trying to find a way out of their arrangement. Not now, not when his career was on the line.

Melody took a breath—the tension in the room was palpable.

"You dirty little pit lizard," were the first words out of her mouth. It made Viv want to try out some of her new self-defense moves on her friend. How could she be joking at a time like this when Jarod's career, his whole livelihood and that of his crew, not to mention millions of dollars, were on the line?

"Why didn't you tell me you were letting Mr. Cage tune your engine?"

"Mel," Viv yelled. "I think that is the last thing we need to be discussing right now."

Mel growled. "Fine. Fine. You'd just think your best friend would let you know when she was getting some. Pretty selfish keeping that tasty bit of information to yourself if you ask me."

"Goddammit." Viv shook her friend. "Focus. What do I

do? He's so close to getting to the Chase. So damn close. It could all be ruined because of me."

"Well, from the looks of these pics, it seems he was very much an active participant. I'd say he took his career into his own hands, Vivi. It's not your fault. "

"Please," Viv said. "I really need your help."

Mel held up a finger and continued to examine the evidence.

"Do you have any idea who's blackmailing you?" She held a photo up to the light.

"The only person I can think of is Gina McKnight."

"Jarod's fiancée?"

"His fake fiancée."

Viv told Mel everything from the moment she met Jarod Cage, filling in all the blanks. She even told her about the last time. When Viv ruined everything between them just because she was scared.

PR Rule Number 13: Two heads are better than one.

"The next morning, I wake up to news that their engagement is back on," Viv said. "He gave me the chance, and I destroyed it. But if these photos get out? He won't recover. His sponsor will pull out and he would become the Tiger Woods of racing. This year would be a memory. All of his work for nothing."

"You think she sees you as a threat? Even after they went public?"

"I don't even know anymore."

"Okay, she'll be at the top of the list. Still, I wonder why she would threaten you, instead of him. Seems she has more pull there. Let's look deeper, who else? Who would want to see you back away from him?"

Viv rattled her brain and then it hit her. Even more

obvious than Gina. Someone who would target her. Who wanted her to quit.

They both said, "Fredrick," at the same time.

"He doesn't have the balls, does he?" Mel asked. "I mean it is weaselly. And getting you off this case would push him up to the New York position. But I'm not sure I see it."

"Yes, yes, yes," Viv said. "He was messing with me from the very beginning. Plus, with a threat like this, he didn't even have to get his hands dirty. Hire a private detective to get the photos. He's such a tech geek, he probably has access to my email. Or maybe he saw us that first day in my office. Someone did knock at the door. Plus, he has the money to send someone off to do his dirty work."

"Okay, let me see what I can find out in the office."

"Does it really even make a difference at this point?"

"Hell yes, it does," Mel said. "Nobody messes around with my girl and gets away with it. When do you have to be back at the track?"

"Thursday." Viv pulled her legs to her chest and rested her chin on her knees. Slowly rocking.

"Okay, hold tight until then." Mel stood and kissed the top of Viv's head. "I think if someone is blackmailing you, they'll be in touch. They haven't made any demands. I think they're just trying to get your attention."

"Well, it worked," she mumbled.

"I know, sweetie." Mel rubbed her back. "Just let me see what I can dig up."

"You're the best," she whispered as her eyes filled.

Viv spent the rest of the day in her pj's watching *Talladega Nights* and *Days of Thunder*. But by the following morning, she wasn't about to take this lying down. She'd make her own luck. Lock her into two choices and she'd come up with three more. They both worked too hard to let some weasel or spoiled brat get their way.

Trouble was, the more time she spent with Jarod on the track, the less and less appealing New York began to look to her.

So she had another idea.

Chapter Twenty-Two

Vi never made it to the Pennsylvania 400. Not for the prerace activities, or for the qualifying. And here they were waiting for the drop of the flag, and there was still no sign of her.

"Listen to me," Henry said down on pit road on race day. "I can't have you sulking over Viv. Not right now. I need your head on tight for this one."

"Fine," Jarod told him. But he felt anything but fine. He kept tugging at the collar of his fire suit, and damn it if he wasn't pacing around like lost puppy.

"Chief," Tim, one of the younger crewmen, said to Henry. He'd been around the tracks from the start of the season, but they'd only hired him to Jarod's pit crew a few weeks ago.

"What?" Henry snapped at the kid, his attention focused on the car's tire pressure. Typically, he was an approachable sort and welcomed input from the crew, but all the guys knew not to interrupt him when he was making the last-minute adjustments.

"We need to go down a pound of air in the left rear," he called out. "What is it, Timmy?"

The lanky kid shuffled his feet. "Inspectors have been sniffing around the garage."

"So," Henry said.

The kid shrugged. "They heard someone's been messing with the fuel in the number nine."

"Ain't nobody been messing with fuel in the number nine." Those were fighting words, especially when shady teams had been banned from racing after putting illegal additives into the fuel. "Who said it, goddamn it? Where the hell did you hear that?"

Henry stopped and swayed. Jarod grabbed his arm.

"Just some rumblings," Tim said. "So I thought I'd let you know before he does his lap."

"Why? Because you think I did something?" Henry sputtered, his face flushing red in anger.

"Shit no," Tim said and took a step back, as if he realized he was out of line. "I just wanted you to know, is all."

"Hey now," Jarod said so low to Henry it was almost a whisper. "No one would ever accuse you of anything. You know that." He didn't spare the new hire a glance.

Henry nodded and straightened away. Jarod watched him closely. Something wasn't…right. "Hey ol' man, you—"

Before he could ask if Henry was all right, the older man clutched his chest, slumping into Jarod's hold.

"What is it?" he asked. But he knew. In his soul, he already knew.

Henry couldn't speak. Jarod carefully lowered him to the ground.

God no. Not now. Not yet.

"Christ, get a medic over here!" Jarod's heart tightened right along with Henry's rigid body. "And you," he pointed to Tim. "Get the fuck out of my garage."

The kid looked at him with his pale face, chewing on his lower lip. It reminded him of something. He'd seen that look before. Tim had been at the bar that night, when he mixed it up with Reddy. Jarod had intended to pick up the kid's tab. He hadn't remembered that until just now, probably because he disappeared from the bar when all the action happened.

God help the kid if he was tampering with anything in his garage, or anyone on his crew.

Henry struggled for breath, and Jarod focused on his friend. He pulled off his jacket to pillow Henry's head. "It's okay, old man. I'm right here. Right here with you. Just hang on. We're getting help."

A medic rushed in and Jarod waved him over.

"Make way," he screamed into the crowd. In the seconds before the medic reached them, Henry's body arched and shuddered and then went eerily still. No. *No*. Jarod thumped Henry's chest, leaned over him and tried to hear if he was breathing.

The medic fell to the ground, paddles in hand, and shoved Jarod aside. He checked Henry's wrist and throat. "No pulse."

Jarod sat back on his haunches as the EMT tore open Henry's shirt before shouting "Clear!" and shocking Henry's lifeless body.

He didn't come to. Three other men carried a stretcher over to his friend. They loaded him up and took him away. It happened so quickly.

It took everything inside Jarod not to break down and

bawl like a goddamn baby.

Roger, Henry's right-hand man, jumped in to take care of the car. He checked the fuel tank and shook his head. "Ain't a goddamn thing wrong with the tank."

"No shit," Jarod said from his position on the ground. He had yet to move. He looked back to see if the ambulance was still in sight. "Like anything would happen on the old man's watch."

The crewmen gathered around Jarod protectively, not so gently encouraging the bystanders and other pit crews to move along and leave them in peace. His crew was family—and they didn't let anyone fuck with the family.

"Jarod." Roger extended a hand and hauled Jarod to his feet. "We've got five minutes left. It's time for your last lap."

It pained him. Motherfucker, he hadn't felt pain like this since his father went into turn two and didn't come out.

"You need to get into your car," Roger told him.

All around him, his crew was moving on as they typically would. There was too much riding on this race, so they would go on. That's just how it went.

"I've got to go with him." Jarod shook his head. "Get me a car."

"J," Roger said, gently. "You can't. Not yet. Henry would fucking kill you if you left right now, and you know it. He'd kill me if I even thought about letting you do such a stupid thing. You listen to me now. He's getting the best care he could be getting. You have to keep moving. You know that. Three races left. Just three, man. You can do this."

• • •

Jarod blew it. There was no sugarcoating it. His performance on the track was a joke.

So when he went to see Henry in the hospital that night, he had no good news. Not that he gave two shits about the race at the moment.

Like most drivers, Jarod hated hospitals, hated them. It was better if he could get through his day without thinking about injury, and sickness, and death. When you lived on the edge, it was best to be fucking delusional about it.

Wheelmen were a superstitious sort. Most would never step a foot in an ER, even if they were bleeding out, let alone visit the ICU. But there was no way Jarod would leave Henry sitting in here alone. Same with his crew.

Sadly, the docs wouldn't them in.

"He's a very sick man, Mr. Cage," the doctor said. "You can have a short visit, but that's it. Nobody else tonight. There will be plenty of time for visitors later. He's not going to be going anywhere anytime soon."

Henry was so doped up on drugs, he didn't even know Jarod was there. He looked so frail lying there in the bed, so old. Jarod pulled up a chair to his bed and held his hand. So what if he shed a tear or two, there was nobody there to witness it.

Jarod stayed until they kicked him out. He expected—shit, he hoped—to see Viv there. He needed a chance to work through all the shit. Who was he kidding? He needed *her*.

She never showed.

Chapter Twenty-Three

After Viv heard about Henry, she was sick with worry. But she couldn't show her face at the hospital when someone could see her. She'd do whatever it took to protect Jarod. And she'd risk everything for him. Not that keeping her distance didn't kill her. She and Mel still had no idea who was blackmailing her, so going to Philly was out of the question. Her heart actually hurt not being able to be there with him. Henry was part of the family, but knowing her stubborn race car driver, he wouldn't want to worry his mother or sister yet. He'd take it all on himself. Alone.

Who was looking out for him? Who was taking care of him?

They were questions that kept her up most of the night.

He was there when his father crashed, and now he was there when his second father had a heart attack right in front of him. And then he was expected to race after all of that. She was sure he didn't even eat or drink enough in the commotion. And did he refuel after? He was probably dangerously close to dehydration.

She was the person to take care of him after the races. That's what she did, and that bothered her more than anything that she wasn't there now. At the time he needed her most.

When she couldn't take it any longer, she called the suits for an update.

"Why aren't you up there, darlin'?" Mr. Fox asked.

"It's a long story, but I had to distance myself from the team. Just for a while. Jarod needs to get to the Chase, and I've became a distraction to him. I couldn't risk it being so close. So I've been working off-site."

"I appreciate that, Viv," Mr. Fox said, unsurprised and really unfazed by the whole thing. "You're a real pro. But is there anything I can do for you? We think the world of you, you know that."

"Actually," she said, deciding to take full advantage of his offer. "There is something."

• • •

Mr. Fox was able to arrange a meeting for Viv at the NASCAR corporate offices the following day. She promised him that if her idea worked, she'd be able to continue with Jarod *and* his other drivers.

Viv killed it in the pitch. Still, they weren't out of the woods yet.

She had to make sure those photos wouldn't surface. She planned to take care of that just as soon as she had the chance to check out Henry for herself.

After her talk with Mr. Fox, she asked if there were a way she could visit Henry on the down low, so she wouldn't create a stir. He arranged some time for her during off-visiting hours.

She went in a side door and up to third floor. Her name was already on the nurses' list. But once she made it into his room, she wasn't at all prepared for the person who sat on the edge of his bed.

Miranda.

She was sitting there, holding his hand. The two were talking in hushed voices, and Viv strained to listen.

"Viv," Henry said before she was able to gather any intel. "Sell my shoes, I've died and gone to heaven. Two beautiful callers on the same day?"

No way to sneak out now.

He looked good. A little pale and tired, but happy. Alive. Viv was relieved.

"Hi, Henry," she said, walking farther into the hospital room. She leaned against the wall opposite his bed. "You gave us quite a scare."

"You know what they say, never a dull moment at the track," he said.

"How are you feeling?" she asked.

"Better," he said. "Much better."

Her boss started to gather up her things, and though Viv wanted to focus all her attention on Henry, she had to find out what was going on. "Miranda, I didn't expect to see you here."

"I'm sure you didn't." It was all she said before kissing Henry good-bye and turning on her heel.

"I didn't know the two of you were so close," Viv said

to Henry.

"Randy and I have known each other for years," Henry said.

Did he just call the Ice Queen Randy?

"It was her idea to put you on the case when I told her I needed someone for Jarod," he continued. "Someone to calm that boy down."

She held up a finger to Henry to signal she'd be right back, and then followed Miranda out the door.

"Miranda," she called, and when her boss didn't stop, Viv jogged down the hallway to stop her. "What did Henry mean when he said he 'needed someone for Jarod'?" she asked.

"Who knows what he's talking about?" She waved her hand. "The man is on Lord knows how many pain pills."

"Was this campaign with Jarod professional or personal?" Viv asked, trying to understand what was going on. "Were you doing a favor for a friend, getting me to take care of Jarod? Or was this about client business?"

"It was a job, Viv," she said. "But I can't control what happens within those parameters."

Odd little alarm bells jingled in her head. The Ice Queen always had agendas. "Did you try to set us up?"

"No," she said. "I just created opportunity. And if that opportunity kept my best employee in Atlanta and helped out a friend, well, so be it."

"That's dirty," she said.

"That's business," Miranda replied. "But I guess that doesn't matter now, does it? I hear you've stepped away from the campaign."

"No," Viv said. "I'm getting ready to finish it."

• • •

The pieces were all falling into place. Viv only had one more big move to make to protect Jarod for good. The only shot she had to fix this mess was to sidle up to Gina. She thought that maybe if they could talk, they could work something out. She was a hell of a negotiator, after all.

So she planned it out for the next few days, discreetly contacting Miss McKnight and requesting a private audience. She specified the place and time, and even worked with Kelsey (her new ally) to make sure that Gina's flights and transportation were arranged. Gina would even be compensated—quite ridiculously—for her visit.

When it was time, Viv flew out to the speedway to end it.

Gina met her at a coffee shop near the track. They took a booth near a window and ordered sweet tea and pie. Though Gina didn't touch it.

The polished woman did not confirm or deny knowing about the photos. She basically just sat and listened. Viv launched into the incriminating evidence and the legal ramifications of attempting to blackmail her or her client. But she made sure to emphasize her desire to find an amicable solution.

"So, you're in love with him?" Gina asked abruptly, interrupting Viv's spiel.

Viv's mouth opened, but no words came out. She placed her forehead in her palm and closed her eyes briefly. She knew there was no point in denying it. She was ready to come clean to everyone. Most importantly, Jarod.

"Yes," she finally admitted.

"And you quit your job for him?" Gina pressed.

That had been the opening line of her conversation. Removing herself from the spotlight. Doing whatever was necessary to eliminate the threat. With Jarod's happiness, his whole future, on the line, the decision had been an easy one. "Yes. Though I found something else."

"Of course," Gina said. "Yankee pride and all that."

"Right." Viv gritted her teeth. "So will you keep the photos to yourself?"

"I'll do what I can to keep them out of the press, but I didn't take these, Viv." She placed a manicured nail on the pile of pictures.

"You didn't?" Shit, she'd been so sure it was Gina. It all lined up.

"No."

"Well, who could it be then?" Viv asked, her mind cycling through the possible suspects.

"Take a number," she said with an elegant shrug. "There is so much money on the line out there, hon. My best guess would be one of the drivers. Who stands to lose the most if Jarod wins? That's who I'd look at. They probably just want to rattle him. Like with the photos, there's no obvious threat. They're just pictures. That's not a crime, but it is a way to rattle him. Or send you away, which is also rattling him. Did you see the results from his last race?"

Viv glanced away. "I think that's due to the situation with Henry more than it is me."

"I wouldn't be so sure of that," she said. "But like I said, I will help in any way I can. But you have to promise me not to go public with your relationship until we officially split."

"That's not going to be a problem," Viv said. Obviously

Gina didn't know he was already through with her. The woman was pragmatic and coldly accommodating. Viv was grateful, but she still didn't trust her. Yes, Gina might act helpful now, but she'd been all too anxious to jump on the Jarod-bashing bandwagon after the incident in the bathroom.

Back to PR Rule Number 1: Know your audience and your enemies. In this case, the latter may be most important.

"I won't be a problem," Gina said. Her expression looked oddly sincere. "This was the last thing I asked of him. He held up his end of the bargain. So my mouth is sealed about his dad's prescription drugs."

"Prescription drugs?" And, what the hell? Just how sealed was her mouth if she was discussing this so openly? Resigned to put out one fire at a time, Viv made a noncommittal sound. "Oh?"

"Yeah, the story that I *didn't* use to make my career. He had to give me something, Viv. Quid pro quo."

Jesus, that's how Jarod's life had always been. Give and take—on the track and off. How could he ever deal with things being uneven? How could he ever trust? And could Viv live without it?

• • •

Once she made her way infield, Viv tried to lie low. She didn't want to mess Jarod up before the race, so she slapped on a baseball cap and sunglasses and tried to blend in with the crowd.

But when she saw Henry walking behind the garages, she couldn't contain herself.

"What are you doing out of the hospital, Henry?" She

ran over to him, scanning the area for Jarod's face, even though she knew she was safe. He'd be down on pit road by now.

"Nothing was going to keep me away from watching my boy get into the Chase," he said, his eyes scanning the area, much like her own.

She just might have a fugitive on her hands. Still, Viv smiled, knowing Jarod would be thrilled he was there.

"But why aren't *you* with him?" Henry asked, as Viv lowered him to the extra lawn chairs one of the crews set up. He looked so much better than he did in the hospital, but not well enough to be out walking around in this heat.

"I would've been there," she said, taking off her hat and gently placing it on Henry's head to shield him from the sun. "There's just so much going on right now."

"What is it, Viv?" he asked. "Where've you been? Does he know you're here?"

Viv broke down and told Henry the whole story. About the photos and Gina, and the entire effed-up mess.

"Then I find out why Jarod let Gina keep him down like that," she said in the wake of the latest discovery. "Did you know?"

"About Tony?" he asked.

"Yes, about Tony," she said, even though she didn't have to. He already answered her question.

"I knew," Henry said. "I also knew it didn't cause the wreck. Sometimes those things happen and there's not a damn thing you can do about it. It sounds scandalous, sounds bad, which is why Jarod wanted to keep it hidden, but it really doesn't matter."

"You might want to tell Jarod that," she said.

"Damn, if I would've known, I would never have let her take him for a ride like that. Not for anything. Not even for Tony. He wouldn't have wanted me to. He wouldn't have wanted that burden on his son. And that move, well, that was her last. We will speak up and we will speak out. I don't care if the kid never talks to me again. This ends now."

"I'm so happy he has you." Viv wiped a tear off her cheek.

"I could say the same," he said. "You really put everything on the line for him. It still could all blow up in your face, you know?"

She swallowed hard. Yeah. "I know."

"He's not going to be happy with that."

"None of that now," she said. "Positive thinking, Henry. He's going to get to the Chase and Miranda's going to accept my deal and everything is going to work out."

"What deal?" Henry asked.

"I can't tell you, Henry, not yet."

"Well there is one thing my boy did have right."

"What's that?"

"You are an infuriating woman, Viv."

"Yeah, yeah, yeah."

"Why don't you get out there and find him," he said. "Tell him to win this thing."

"You don't think that will get him too rattled?"

"Of course it will get him rattled." He winked. "Get out there."

Viv made her way through the infield as the guys were taking the warm-up laps. She had one chance to talk to him. But someone else grabbed her attention first.

Charlie's wife, Alisha.

Viv almost called out to her, until she saw who she was meeting behind the black motor coach. One of the dirtiest crew chiefs on the circuit. Reddy's crew chief. Something wasn't right, and Viv couldn't silence Gina's words ringing in her ears.

It's one of the drivers.

Viv knew the stats of all the racers backward and forward. And the driver most threatened by Jarod was…Charlie.

No, not another betrayal.

She followed them as they huddled by the RV, and crept around to the other side, so she could hear the exchange.

"Here's the first half," Alisha said to Reddy's man. "But you need to wreck him good. You'll get the other half after the race, but only if the number nine can't cross the finish line."

"It's done," he said, and Viv's stomach turned. The image of Jarod's car crashing had bile rising up her throat.

By the time she rounded the corner to confront Alisha, Reddy's guy was gone.

"I can't believe Charlie would do this to his friend," she said to this woman who invited her into her home. This scum who was trying to destroy the man she loved.

And she did love him.

It was all starting to make sense. The photos. The accusations against Henry. Even the sex tape. She was sure it all came from one source.

"Viv," Alisha said, trying to regain her composure. "What are you doing here?"

"Listening to you bribe a driver into wrecking Jarod."

"Hang on there, Viv," she said. "You must've misunderstood."

"How could you guys do this to him?" she asked.

"Don't bring Charlie into this," she snapped, taking a step closer. "He's done nothing wrong."

"Yeah, I'm sure you covered his tracks." Viv stood her ground. "But I'll find them. You can count on it."

Viv's heart ached. Between his father and Gina, Henry's heart attack, and the way she left, she wasn't sure he'd ever recover from this latest blow. Charlie was his closest friend on the circuit.

She couldn't think about any of that right now; she had to warn him. Taking care of Jarod was her first priority, but making the Stewarts pay for this was a close second.

And, oh yes, there would be hell to pay.

Chapter Twenty-Four

It was the last race before moving on to the Chase, and Jarod needed a big win. Without Henry and Viv in his corner, his record was shot to hell. He had to race this one perfectly.

Not an easy task when his head ached and his concentration was shit.

The past few weeks had been too much solitude—even for his reclusive ass. Too much thinking, pining, dreaming. As it turned out, there were people he needed just as much—more, in fact—as those who needed him. A breakthrough he didn't take lightly.

And he'd had a lot of breakthroughs over the past few months. Vi's yoga teacher would call it *enlightenment.* How sad was it when he missed her silly stories about her yogi. He tried calling her the day she left. He tried texting. He even took to writing, which frankly was more his speed. She replied only once saying she couldn't talk to him. Not yet.

It was the last part he was clinging to.

He hoped she'd agree to meet with him after the race. God, he had so much to tell her. If she wouldn't oblige, he wasn't above begging.

He'd worked out so much shit in the past two weeks. The biggest development was: no more Gina. If she wanted to make her mark with his father's dirty laundry, he couldn't stop her. He wouldn't.

But he wanted to come clean to Vi before Gina had her say. He just hoped she'd listen. Jarod talked to his mother about the allegations against his dad. Not just allegations, the fucking proof. Turns out his mom knew the whole time.

Here he was keeping these secrets, trying to control everything. For what? For whom?

"You don't need to protect him anymore, honey," his mom had said. "You don't need to protect me, either. We're a tough lot, and you don't need to carry us on your shoulders. Let us take a turn and carry you."

He wasn't sure he could do that, but he was willing to try. Jesus, the past few weeks had been like a goddamn therapy session. He had too much time to think, too much time to come to the conclusion he'd been a complete idiot. His views on so many things were warped. Even what he initially thought of as Viv's biggest betrayal, he now understood was actually her way of protecting him, because she cared.

The question was, did she still?

He wasn't sure what he'd do if she didn't, because he was in love with the gorgeous Yank. And after this race, he was going to do everything in his power to take their once-temporary solution and make it permanent. All she had to do was say yes.

There was nothing standing in their way now, and if he

had to move his base to the Big Apple, so be it.

"Just like we talked about, J-boy," Roger said in his headset, jerking him back to reality. Time to get a grip. He had a lot of work ahead of him before he could drop to one knee.

Roger's voice was a calming force as Jarod took his practice laps. He was no Henry, but Rog worked his ass off, and Jarod trusted him 100 percent.

"How's it feeling out there?" Roger asked.

"Feels good," Jarod said. "Real good. The car's not pulling like it was."

"Henry helped me with that one," Roger said.

"Damn, I wish he was here."

"He's watching every second, J. You know he is."

"I know," Jarod said. He accelerated into the next turn. "And you and I make a great team. It's just that the old guy would've gotten such a charge out of this."

"So give him a show," Roger said.

• • •

Jarod lapped for the final time before the start. He was energized. He was ready.

And before he knew it, the track roared to life. Jarod was completely in the zone when the green flag dropped.

He had tried for the pole for this race, but didn't come close. That lead position really could've helped him. But it was okay. He'd take it one lap at a time.

He made the first few laps and found his groove. He came up on Charlie, gave him a nod and made a clean pass, which was more than he could say for the dirty racing going on with Reddy's team.

The asshole clipped him earlier, but Jarod always avoided him at all cost. He anticipated his cheap shots.

Jarod's car lunged forward after a wicked tap from behind.

What the fuck?

Charlie was bumping him, trying to push him into Reddy, who was hugging him on the other side. Since when was Charlie tag-teaming with Reddy?

He kept the car straight, but wasn't able to do much more than that.

"Down low," Roger said, seeing the trap.

"Not sure I can get there," Jarod said. "They're killing me out here, Rog."

Why was Charlie doing this? He didn't race this way.

It was then that he heard that punk Tim's words in his head. "It's not just me," the kid said after Jarod fired him from the crew after he nearly killed Henry. "It's not just me."

Of course at the time, he figured Tim was talking about Reddy. But maybe there were more. Could his friend be involved? His mind raced. Charlie did know all his secrets when it came to Gina, and…Candace. Candace was Charlie's wife's best friend.

This was so messed up.

"J-boy," a familiar voice rang in his ear, bringing everything into focus.

Henry.

"Those motherfuckers are trying to wreck you," Henry said. "Stay clear of ten and four. You hear me?"

"What the hell are you doing?" he asked, not understanding a thing that was going on down on pit road—or on the fucking track. Was Henry here? Or did they patch him in?

"I'm here to get you out of this shitstorm," Henry said.

Jarod had never been happier to hear a voice in his life.

"Now you don't worry about the hows and whys. Viv and I have that under control."

"Viv?" Reddy rammed him so hard, Jarod's teeth clanged together. His front end was shaking, pulling to the right.

Keep the car on the road, Cage. That's all you have to do.

"Yeah, your girl is here, too. She told me to tell you she'll be back after she *goes all Tammy and Patsy* on Charlie's wife—whatever the hell that means."

Go get her, Vi.

He wasn't sure what was going on, and he didn't want to believe that Charlie was trying to fuck him over. But as Henry said, don't worry about the hows and whys right now. He just needed to trust them.

"Now I want you to break away when you can and stay low," he said. "The car can handle it."

"I don't know," Jarod said, his eyes moving from the dash to the low side of the track.

"You listen to me," Henry said. "Break away now!"

He did as he was told. He punched it and dropped low, getting out of the Charlie-Reddy sandwich. And he pulled away from the pack.

It was working.

And for the next two hours and forty minutes, he listened to Henry and followed his instincts. He gutted himself, fighting for position in every lap. He even took a few helpful taps from Lach. Henry was with him for every second, and Viv was out there somewhere raising hell on his behalf.

It's what got him to the finish…in first place.

• • •

Jarod didn't waste a second after he crossed the finish line. He pushed his way through a sea of people, trying to get a visual on her, ignoring the cameras and reporters along the way.

They were used to that. He would deal with them later; right now he desperately needed to see her face.

"Vi," he mouthed once they locked eyes. She was with Henry, and the sight of her made him ache. He was sure the fans were expecting him to go after Charlie or Reddy, but he'd let the suits handle those assholes.

He just needed to get to Vi.

She pushed her way to him, and they finally met in the center of the crowd. He reached out to her, but she narrowed her eyes, shaking her head. He knew the press would have a field day with any move he made toward her, especially after Gina's stunt. He didn't care.

But the point was, Vi cared. And she also had a reputation to protect. If things were going to work between them, he couldn't always be the guy calling the shots.

So he waited.

Chapter Twenty-Five

Viv wanted nothing more than to lock her arms around the gorgeous man standing in front of her in his fire suit. And she wanted to stay there until the sun went down, but she couldn't risk it. Everything was out of control and messed up. There was no time for celebration. Not yet.

Her hands itched to touch him to make sure he was safe, and that he was really there with her. She allowed one hand to graze his arm, and he instantly placed his own hand over hers and squeezed. By that simple gesture, she knew everything was going to be okay.

Immediately after Jarod made it through the media circus, she went with him and Henry to a meeting with the racing executives and their investigative team in the motorized offices on the inside track.

And then the three of them proceeded to tell the whole disgusting story.

Jarod told them about all the connections to the

Stewarts. His theory about Candace and the way Tim hinted that there were more people involved. And Viv added in the information about the photos she was being blackmailed with and, more importantly, what she saw and heard with Reddy and Alisha.

Henry shared the accusations made about the fuel tampering in the garage. It was enough, more than enough, and it wasn't long before the execs got the local authorities involved and issued arrest warrants.

It was dark by the time they were through, and they were all too exhausted to say another word as they walked Henry to the garage. He said there'd be someone there to take him home.

She didn't expect it to be Miranda.

"You fool," her boss said, looking over Henry like a mother hen. "What were you thinking coming down here?"

"I had to see him do it," he told her, pulling the Ice Queen into a corner. "I had to."

"So *they* know each other?" Jarod asked.

"Oh yeah," Viv said. "They know each other, all right."

"Babe, I want to hear all about it, I really do, and I know we have so much to figure out, but I can't wait any longer. If I don't get you in the bus in the next ten seconds, your boss is going to get an eyeful."

"I'm not sure if she's still my boss," Viv said.

"After all of this," he spat, "the hell she isn't."

Viv put a hand to his face, trying to soothe. "Just give me another minute," she said. This was the final piece to the puzzle. And then they would have all the time they needed.

"Miranda," she said, walking over to where she stood with Henry. "I know you have to get him home, but this won't take long."

"Okay." Miranda folded her arms across her chest. "Hurry up, then."

"I fulfilled my end of the bargain," she said. "I helped get Jarod to the Chase."

"And now you're ready to move on to New York?" Miranda asked, and Viv noticed there were bags under her eyes and she was paler than usual. "Fine, if that's what you want. I won't go back on my word."

"That's not what I want."

"Thank Christ," Jarod said on an exhale.

"I'd like to stay with Elite," she said, reaching for Jarod's hand. He took it without delay. "But I have a proposition for you."

"Go on." Miranda raised an eyebrow in that condescending way of hers.

"I've recently discovered that NASCAR has a need for a PR agency," she said. "They're looking for people who really know the ins and outs of racing. And they want to work with Elite."

"Why do I detect an *if* coming after that sentence?" Miranda asked.

Viv just went for it. "*If* I oversee the program, working a little closer to their corporate headquarters."

"I see," Miranda said, not giving anything away. "Let me get Henry home and think on it. I trust you have a proposal letter and contract."

"I do," she said.

She really didn't, but she'd get one before Miranda made it back to Atlanta.

"Okay then, I'll have an answer for you shortly."

• • •

"What does this mean, Vi?" Jarod asked once Miranda and Henry left. His hands were shaking, and his head was light.

"I'm giving us options," she said. "So we can really make a go of it."

"And you're willing to give up New York for me?" he asked, pulling her closer.

"For us," she said. "But for the record, I don't think I'm giving up a thing."

"So there is an *us*?" he asked. "A future? After all that's happened?"

"There's always been an us," she said. "And I have to tell you—"

He stopped her before she could go off on one of her tangents, hauling her up against him to take liberties with her mouth. He crushed his lips on hers with a kiss that said everything he'd been feeling since the moment he walked into her office.

"Vivian Blake," he finally said when he was able to pull away, "I love you."

"I love you, too," she said in that adorable Yankee voice of hers.

His damn heart sang. He'd been given a second chance, and he wasn't going to blow it. He stepped back and picked her up, depositing her on the hood of his car.

"In that case, I have a proposition of my own," he said as he went rummaging through the toolboxes. "Of course, I'd like to do this proper, and I haven't had time to shop. But there will be time for that later."

"What are you talking about, Jarod?" she asked.

"You're going to need to go with your instincts on this one," he said when he found a silver washer about the right size. Then he walked over to her and placed the flat ring at the tip of her finger. "I hope this will do, because, baby, you are the only option I will ever need. Will you marry me?"

Epilogue

Viv bounced off the walls waiting for her friend to arrive. She wanted Mel to love everything she did about Cotton Creek. She hoped that she would visit during the racing off-season. Of course Viv would continue to make her own trips to Atlanta whenever she could. Miranda insisted on it.

She let her boss take the credit for the NASCAR contract. Turns out her newly found negotiation skills had nothing on the Ice Queen. But with the money the contract brought in to Elite, Viv's position there was secure. She wished she could say the same for Mel.

Miranda was riding her as hard as ever; that's why Viv had suggested a weekend in the country. Mel had jumped at the chance.

Viv paced around the den, dusting Jarod's Sprint Cup for the hundredth time. You'd think she had won the thing the way she cared for it. Then she moved on to the photos of the two of them in *USA Today* and the *New York Post.* Jarod insisted her awards get the same treatment. And boy did she hit the mother lode after Jarod won the Sprint Cup. It was a PR jackpot.

There was also the press that they didn't want, especially when word leaked about the Reddy/Stewart arrests. Still, they faced it head-on. They'd come too far to go into hiding. But not too far to have compassion. It didn't take long for Candace's name to come up in connection with the Stewarts. She was indeed part of the ruse, but she came clean. As it turned out, she was in love with Jarod and not at all happy with the arrangement they had over the years. She felt used, worth nothing, so when Charlie's wife came to her with an idea—and a large payout—she took the deal.

Jarod realized he had to shoulder some of the responsibility and come to terms with the fact that he had used people, just as they used him.

Still, he didn't forgive Candace easily, but once she gave her statement and apologized over and over again in every way possible, his anger began to dissipate. They were able to get her off without any charges. Viv firmly believed it was the right thing to do.

Gosh, it all seemed so long ago—they had moved on, leaving those bad parts of their love story in the past. Focusing on only the good.

Jarod came up from behind her now, snaking his arms around her waist, whispering filth in her ear. Those good parts never got old.

Everything had fallen into place, and it took the least amount of planning. What's that saying? Life happens when you're busy making other plans. Well, that's exactly what happened to Viv. And she refused to miss a minute of it.

Things weren't perfect. Some of the guys at work complained that she had preferential treatment because of her fiancé. But she wasn't worried.

Once they saw what she could do, there would be no question about why she was there. It was her dream job. The dream she never knew she wanted. Traveling across the country with one of the fastest-growing sports organizations in the world…with her fiancé. Followed by a few days off in quaint Cotton Creek to recharge. Plus Mrs. B's cornbread and grits whenever she wanted? It was perfect.

Her new version of perfect.

The phone rang, and she reluctantly left Jarod's arms to answer it.

"Vivi," Mel's voice rang out on the other end. "I'm so sorry, but I can't make it this weekend. I would've called earlier, but I've been stuck with the Ice Queen for the last four hours."

"What happened?" she asked, her heart dropping to feet. If her boss was involved, it couldn't be good. And she'd been looking forward to spending time with her friend for weeks.

"Long story," Mel said. "But I have a huge new client, and Miranda's on my ass like you wouldn't believe. All this talk about going with instinct and commitment to my career and blah, blah, blah."

Viv fingers went itchy—suddenly, she was having a very strange sense of déjà vu.

"Who is the client?" she asked, suspicious.

"A country artist, actually," Mel said with a quiver.

"Mmm-hmm," she said. "And what does this country artist look like?"

Jarod shot her a quick glare. Not liking where this line of questioning was going.

"Oh, I don't know." A nervous laugh fell from Mel's lips. "Like a cowboy, I guess."

Damn, Viv couldn't be sure, but it sure sounded like Miranda Wells was up to something again. More matchmaking, or just executing a new part of her employee retention program? She didn't know. But she had the feeling that Mel was going to find out very soon.

"Well, you be careful with that, hon," she said before Jarod stalked over to her. "I've heard cowboys are even more dangerous than race car drivers." And with that, she hung up before Jarod launched himself at her.

"Cowboys are more dangerous, huh?" He captured her mouth in a possessive kiss, cupped his hands on her ass, and lifted, hiking her legs up and around his waist. "Well, good thing Mel's visit is postponed."

"Why?" she asked as he walked them toward the bedroom, her insides turning to mush as they always did when he touched her.

"Because I plan on making your reconsider your position on that…actually, I plan on making your reconsider many positions now that we have an entire weekend to kill."

"You think so?" she said, always trying to play hardball with him. "PR Rule Number 5: Actions speak louder than words."

"Absolutely," he agreed. "And baby, I plan on being very, very loud."

Acknowledgments

Bringing this book into the world was a long race with many left turns. But once I got going, it was like a ride with Jarod Cage—fast and insanely exciting!

My agent, Jessica Sinsheimer, was the very first person to *get Caged* and her enthusiasm for this story really kept me going, so many thanks go out to her.

I'm also so thankful for Heather Howland, who was incredible during this entire process. She not only said yes to *this* book, but asked, "How many do you have in the series?" Thank you for welcoming me into the Entangled family and for taking so much time with me during those first few weeks.

Vanessa Mitchell is an editorial goddess. She really helped shape this book and encouraged me to go deep with this one. And just by reading her edits, I knew she really *got* me. She also kept me laughing during our challenging schedule. I'm so grateful for her!

To Anita, Curtis, Debbie, Erin, and the entire Entangled

team—I am so impressed by your professionalism and dedication to your books. Thanks so much for everything… and answering all my annoying questions.

Thanks to Heidi Joy Tretheway for reading those first messy pages, saying such great things, and giving me awesome (and dirty) advice for my boy, Jarod.

To Danielle and Cameron at Barclay Publicity—so excited to have you both on the team. I'm looking forward to doing great things together.

Huge hugs also go out to my readers. I love that you guys send me notes and funny comments out on social media. You are amazing and make this journey so worth it.

Finally, to my family and friends—why are you guys always last? Because you're the best, of course. Thanks for your patience with me when I'm on deadline (which is always), and being around for shenanigans when I'm not. I'm so lucky to have each one of you in my life.

And to my guys at home who bring me so much joy—there aren't enough books in the world to explain what you both mean to me. Cheesy, right? Sorry, but that's how I feel. My husband is extraordinary and has kept our entire household running while I've been locked away in my writing cave. Seriously, I could NOT do it without him. And the kiddo? There are no words. I love you guys!

About the Author

A fan of spunky women, gorgeous guys, and super-hot romance, Clare James spends most of her time lost in books. When she's not reading, you can find her locked away writing her own steamy stories.

Clare is also a former dancer and still loves to get her groove on—mostly to work off her beloved cupcakes and red wine. She lives in Minneapolis with her two leading men—her husband and young son—and is always on social media chatting with readers.

Find her at:
www.clarejamesbooks.com
@clarejamesbooks
http://www.facebook.com/clarejamesauthor

www.ingramcontent.com/pod-product-compliance
Lightning Source LLC
La Vergne TN
LVHW091037080826
845145LV00002B/535

* 9 7 8 1 9 4 3 3 3 6 5 2 4 *